Dear Reader,

Looking back over the years, I find it hard to realise that twenty-six of them have gone by since I wrote my first book — *Sister Peters in Amsterdam*. It wasn't until I started writing about her that I found that once I had started writing, nothing was going to make me stop — and at that time I had no intention of sending it to a publisher. It was my daughter who urged me to try my luck.

I shall never forget the thrill of having my first book accepted. A thrill I still get each time a new story is accepted. Writing to me is such a pleasure, and seeing a story unfolding on my old typewriter is like watching a film and wondering how it will end. Happily of course.

To have so many of my books re-published is such a delightful thing to happen and I can only hope that those who read them will share my pleasure in seeing them on the bookshelves again. . .and enjoy reading them.

Back by Popular Demand

A collector's edition of favourite titles from one of the world's best-loved romance authors. Mills & Boon are proud to bring back these sought after titles and present them as one cherished collection.

BETTY NEELS: COLLECTOR'S EDITION

A GIRL IN A MILLION

BY
BETTY NEELS

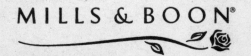

MILLS & BOON®

*First published in Great Britain 1993 by Mills & Boon Limited
This edition 1998
Harlequin Mills & Boon Limited,
Eton House, 18-24 Paradise Road, Richmond, Surrey TW9 1SR*

© Betty Neels 1993

ISBN 0 263 81180 8

*Set in Times Roman 10½ on 13 pt by
Rowland Phototypesetting Limited
Bury St Edmunds, Suffolk*

12-9806-52000

*Printed and bound in Spain
by Litografia Rosés S.A., Barcelona*

CHAPTER ONE

THE thin spring sunshine had little warmth and the pale blue sky looked cold, but together they turned the row of old gabled houses into a charming picture. They faced a narrow canal, tree-lined, the water dark, the arched bridge at its end leading to a street busy with traffic.

The girl walking along the narrow pavement paused to look about her and then, studying the street plan she was carrying, hitched the small package she held under one arm and crossed the narrow street to stand under the budding trees and study the houses opposite.

They were impressive, two and three storeys high with small windows in their various gables, heavy front doors with fanlights above them and with a double flight of steps leading to the door. Some of them had numbers on their walls; one or two had a coat-of-arms carved in stone above the fanlight.

Satisfied, she crossed the street again and mounted the steps of a tall house with high wide windows on each side of its door and an impressive gable, and thumped at the heavy knocker.

The man who opened the door was old, very thin

and very upright with a fringe of white hair and pale blue eyes. He was dressed neatly in a black alpaca jacket and striped trousers and he addressed her in civil tones but, unfortunately, in Dutch.

She held out the packet she had been carrying. 'I'm sorry, I don't understand Dutch. This is for Mr van Houben, from Corinna.'

The elderly face slowly wrinkled into a smile. 'I will see that he receives it, miss. Do you wish to give your name?'

'No—no, thank you. Corinna asked me to deliver it here since I was coming to Amsterdam.' She smiled nicely. 'How very well you speak English.'

He gave a grave inclination of the head. 'Thank you, miss.'

'Well, goodbye.' She smiled again and went down the steps. She ran down the bottom one as a dark blue Bentley drew up. She turned her head to look at it, took a step which wasn't there, and fell in an untidy heap on to the pavement.

She wasn't hurt, she assured herself, and then said so to the enormous man crouching beside her. 'So silly of me,' she added politely.

He took no notice of that. 'Arms and legs all right?' he asked, and it seemed perfectly natural that his English should be as good as her own. 'You have a graze on your arm—any pains anywhere?'

When she said no, he heaved her gently to her feet, dusted her down and urged her back up the steps.

'I've just been there,' she told him. 'There's no need to bother anyone—I'm quite all right…!'

He had bright blue eyes in a handsome face dominated by a powerful nose. He studied her now, standing on the step by the door. 'You need a wash and your hair could do with a comb.' His voice was impersonal but kind.

The colour came into her face, made pale by the shock of falling: A pretty girl, she reflected bitterly, could get away with that, but she couldn't, she hadn't the looks—a small tip-tilted nose, a wide, generous mouth and a great deal of light brown hair didn't amount to much, although her eyes were beautiful; grey, thickly fringed. She held her tongue and allowed herself to be ushered back up the steps and into the house.

The hall was impressive and so typical of the Dutch Interior paintings she had been at pains to study at the Rijksmuseum that for a moment she wondered if this house was a museum too. Apparently not. She listened without understanding while there was an exchange of Dutch over her head and the elderly man went away, to return in a moment with a middle-aged woman with a formidable bosom and a kind face who clucked over her in a kindly fashion and led her away to the back of the hall and into a cloakroom secreted behind the dark panelling, the very antithesis of the hall: comfort—no, luxury with its elegant fittings, thickly carpeted floor and mirrored walls and a shelf full of just about everything needed to improve one's appearance. The girl washed her face and hands and the quite nasty graze on her arm and, since there was no help for it, took the pins out of her hair and combed it with one of the ivory combs on the shelf, and pinned it neatly again. A little lipstick and powder would have been nice, but she didn't like to use any of these, arranged so beguilingly on the shelf.

She looked awful, she decided, and went back into the hall, to the stout woman who led her into a room on the other side of the splendid staircase.

There was another unintelligible exchange of Dutch before she was asked to sit down.

'I'll take a look at that graze,' said her host, and, having done so, went and rummaged in a black bag on the enormous desk under the window, to return with gauze and strapping and a tube of something.

'A soothing ointment,' he explained, and added, 'Keep it covered for a couple of days.' When he had finished he asked, 'You know Corinna?! Fram tells me that the parcel you were kind enough to bring is from her.'

The graze felt much better but she was aware of several sore spots on other parts of her person. 'Yes, I know her…'

'You are a nurse too?'

'I'm not trained yet. Corinna has almost finished, but we've been working on the same ward.'

'Will you tell her that I'm delighted to have the

book?' He had gone to sit behind his desk. 'I had better introduce myself—Marius van Houben.'

She said gravely, 'How do you do? I'm Caroline Frisby. Thank you for your kindness and you saw to my graze quite expertly; lots of people have no idea what to do even for the simplest cut.'

'One does one's best,' murmured her host. 'May I offer you a cup of coffee?'

She got to her feet. 'No, thank you, I must get back: there's a tour of the city this afternoon and I should like to go on it.'

He went to open the door and Fram was waiting in the hall. She shook hands, thanked the butler for opening the door, and went carefully down the steps and walked briskly away, very aware of the tender spots on her small, too thin person.

It was quite a long way back to the hotel, but she had plenty of time. Aunt Meg had intended to do some shopping and had arranged to meet her at noon, when the hotel would provide them with coffee and sandwiches. It was a small hotel squashed into a narrow street near the Amstel River, very clean, the bedrooms small but the beds comfortable, serving a breakfast of rolls and cheese and jam and coffee each morning, coffee and sandwiches again if needed at midday and a substantial meal at night to its guests, who were for the most part quiet middle-aged couples with not much money to spend, content to roam the streets of the city, explore the museums and churches and gaze into shop windows. Caroline had come with her aunt because that lady hadn't liked the idea of going alone although she was determined to explore Amsterdam, a city she had always wished to visit. Caroline, with two weeks' holiday due, had willingly agreed to go with her; Aunt Meg had given her a home when her parents had died within a few weeks of each other of a particularly virulent flu. Not only had she done that, she had made her welcome, treated her as a daughter, strained her resources to have her educated and, when Caroline had decided that she would like to be a nurse, had encouraged her to leave the small house at Basing, a small village to the east of Basingstoke, and enrol at one of the London teaching hospitals. She had been there almost eighteen months now, and although she still missed the quiet life of the village it wasn't too far for her to go back there twice a month.

Her aunt was waiting for her, a comfortable matronly figure, sensibly clad in various shades of brown.

'Well?' she wanted to know. 'Did you find the house?'

'Yes, Aunt. It was one of those patrician town houses beside one of the small canals branching off from the Herengracht.'

'Who answered the door?'

'I suppose he was a butler. He was very polite and he spoke English.' She paused. 'I fell down the steps as I left. The cousin of Corinna's who was to have the package picked me up and put something on a graze…'

'Did you like him?' Aunt Meg never beat about the bush.

'Well, he seemed very nice—kind, you know, and lovely manners. I felt a fool.'

'One always does. Never mind, dear, you're not likely to meet him again. Let us go and eat our sandwiches; I'm looking forward to this tour.'

The coach, with its guide, took them around the city: the Oude Kerk, the Nieuwe Kerk, the Koninklijk Paleis, a bewildering succession of museums, Anne Frankhuis and, finally, the Rijksmuseum. Caroline, a sensible girl, aware that she might never get the chance to see Amsterdam again, listened and looked and stored away a multitude of odd sights and sounds to think about later, and in between whiles she thought about Corinna's cousin. He had looked like a man of leisure and he lived in a splendid house; probably he did nothing much—sat on a few committees perhaps, lent his name to boards of directors. She didn't know Corinna well enough to ask. It was only by chance that Corinna had got to hear that she was going to Amsterdam and had asked her to take the package and deliver it. 'It's only books,' she had said, 'but they cost the earth to post and they might get lost…'

There was a trip to Alkmaar on the following day

but her Aunt Meg hadn't had her fill of Amsterdam
yet. She spent the day wandering up and down the
narrow lanes and streets and Caroline, nothing loath,
went with her. They got lost several times but that,
as her aunt pointed out, was half the fun. It was a
pity that their wanderings took them nowhere near the
Herengracht; Caroline, keeping her eyes open for a
dark blue Bentley, saw no sign of it.

It was a good thing, she told herself firmly, that
they would be going back home on the following day.

Their return home was made on a drab and chilly
day, a remnant of winter. From the coach windows
Holland looked flat and dull and very wet, but
England looked dull too, even if not as flat, as they
sped Londonwards from the ferry. Caroline had two
more days' holiday before she had to return to hospital, so once they reached Victoria and wished their
fellow passengers goodbye she and Aunt Meg were
able to take themselves off to catch the next train to
Basingstoke and from there get a taxi for the two
miles to Basing.

Aunt Meg had shopped prudently in Amsterdam,
with forethought, and while Caroline lit the fire in the
sitting-room and carried their cases upstairs to the two
small bedrooms her aunt opened a Dutch can of soup,
warmed rolls in the oven and made a pot of tea.

Tea made, they ate at the kitchen table since it was
already evening and the journey had been tiring. 'Not
that the coach wasn't comfortable,' observed Aunt

Meg, 'and everyone in it very pleasant, but it's not the same as going on your own, is it?' She smiled across the table at Caroline. 'We could have done with that Bentley car you were telling me about—now that's the way to travel.'

Caroline, spooning the thick Dutch soup, agreed. The memory of Marius van Houben was still vivid; it was also a waste of time. 'We'll unpack in the morning,' she told her aunt. 'There'll be time to get the washing and ironing done before I go back.'

She was up early to make tea, load the washing machine and then go into the garden to take a look around her. Another week or so and it would be April; her aunt's flower-beds were bursting with green shoots and the rhubarb was coming along nicely under its bucket. It was a bit early to go across the street and collect Theobald, Aunt Meg's cat who had been boarded out while they were abroad, so she contented herself with poking around the seedlings in the tiny greenhouse before going back indoors and setting the table for their breakfast.

The meal over, she filled the washing-line at the end of the garden and went across to Mrs Parkin's for Theobald. The sun had come out now, and the village, so peaceful and quiet despite its nearness to Basingstoke, looked delightful. She paused to admire the small houses and cottages around her before thumping on Mrs Parkin's door knocker.

Theobald, an elderly tabby with a torn ear and

handsome whiskers, was pleased to see her. 'Good as gold,' avowed Mrs Parkin. 'Got 'is wits about 'im, 'e 'as. 'As you 'ad a nice time in foreign parts?'

'Lovely, thank you, Mrs Parkin. Aunt Meg will be over to see you presently and she will tell you all about it.'

Caroline bore the cat back to his own home, pegged out the rest of the washing and, with her aunt having a chat over the coffee-cups with Mrs Parkin, took herself off to the village stores. There were several customers there, all of whom she knew, and all of whom wanted to know if the holiday had been a success.

'Historically a most interesting city,' observed the vicar's wife, who prided herself on being cultured. 'Of course you visited all the museums and art galleries?'

'Well, as many as we could cram in,' said Caroline, 'and we walked around, just looking, you know—some of the houses are very beautiful…'

'Now, you can't beat an Italian villa,' chimed in Miss Coates, who lived alone in a large house at the end of the village and went to Italy each spring, and enlarged upon the subject until she had been served with half a pound of butter, a tin of sardines, and half a dozen stamps from the Post Office end of the shop.

When she had gone Mrs Reece, who owned the shop said, 'Now she's gone, do tell us, Caroline, did you meet anyone nice?'

Everyone there knew that she meant a young man. 'Well, no, the other people on the trip were middle-aged couples, and two schoolteachers…'

'You must have met a lot of people—in the street, I mean,' persisted Mrs Reece, who had a fondness for Caroline and would have liked to see her married.

'I did meet one person—I had to deliver a parcel…' Caroline related her visit to the magnificent house by the canal and her tumble. 'I felt a fool,' she ended, 'and I ruined a pair of tights.'

'Was he very handsome?' asked Mrs Reece.

'Oh, yes, very—and tall and big.'

'"Ships that pass in the night",' the vicar's wife quoted, 'One so often meets a person one would wish to know better if one had the opportunity.' She handed Mrs Reece a list of groceries, 'I remember when we were in Vienna…'

Caroline was the last customer. 'Well, dearie, I'm glad you enjoyed yourself, though it's a shame that there weren't any young folk around.'

Never mind the young folk, reflected Caroline, in-specting the cheeses, Mr Marius van Houben would do very nicely.

That day and the next went all too quickly. She took a late afternoon bus to Basingstoke and got on the train, hanging out of the window until the last minute, waving to Aunt Meg. She would be back again in two weeks' time for her days off but at the moment she derived little comfort from that. She hated going back and yet once she was there, in the hospital, busy on the ward, she was happy.

The nurses' home, a grim appendage to the hospital, looked bleak from the outside, but inside it was cheerful enough, and although the rooms were decidedly small they were nicely furnished and there were three sitting-rooms, one for the sisters, one for trained staff and one for the student nurses. Caroline poked her nose round the door of the last mentioned and was greeted by several girls lounging around reading and drinking tea.

They begged her to put her case down and tell them all about her holiday while she drank a mug of tea, unpacked the cake her aunt had made for her and handed it round.

'Meet any nice men?' asked one of the girls, Janey, a pretty fair-haired girl.

'No—at least, I did meet one, I'm not sure if he was nice…'

She had everyone's attention. 'Do tell…'

She told and when she had finished Janey exclaimed. 'You could have fainted or burst into tears, you know—captured his attention.' She sighed. 'Really, Caro—for a woman of twenty-four you're hopeless at catching the male eye!'

'I didn't feel faint, and you know how hideous I look if I cry.'

There was a protesting chorus telling her that she

hadn't needed to feel faint; just to look pale and help-less would have done very well.

Caroline said meekly that she would know what to do next time, with the secret thought that being pale and helpless would cut no ice with a man like Mr van Houben. His eyes, compellingly blue though they were, were razor-sharp.

She went on duty the next morning, back to Women's Surgical, chock-a-block since it was take-in week, with beds down the centre of the ward and several disgruntled ladies forced to sleep in Women's Medical where they had beds empty.

'It's a funny state of affairs,' observed Staff Nurse James, deftly shortening a tube and putting on a fresh dressing while Caroline handed things and made cheerful remarks to the nervous patient. 'Here's us bursting at the seams, and two whole wards closed because there's no money to keep them open. There, that's done, Mrs Crisp, and I'm sure you'll feel more comfortable now. Clear away, will you, Nurse, and then go and get your coffee?'

Corinna was in the canteen and as Caroline went in she called her over to the table where she was sitting. 'Did you find the house?' she wanted to know. 'I hope it wasn't too much of a nuisance for you? I'm very grateful—the book was far too precious to send by post—a first edition. Thanks awfully. Did you have a good time?'

'Yes, delightful, thank you.' Corinna, she thought,

was very like her cousin; her eyes were bright blue too, although her nose was a delicate beak, which rather added to her good looks. If she had known Corinna better she might have told her that she had met her cousin; as it was, she went and got her coffee and sat down at another table with several of her friends.

She was tired by the time she went off duty at six o'clock; there had been two emergency admissions who had gone to Theatre during the day and one of the student nurses had gone off sick during the afternoon, which meant that two of them were doing the work of three.

Caroline kicked off her shoes, made a cheerful telephone call to Aunt Meg and curled up with a book in the sitting-room. Exercise in the fresh air was essential to a nurse's well being, Sister Tutor had been telling decades of students that, but Caroline decided that her day had provided enough exercise, and anyway the air, laden with fumes from the never-ending traffic of the East End of London, wasn't fresh. The book, she decided after ten minutes' reading, was dull, so she closed it and allowed her thoughts to wander.

The holiday in Amsterdam had been a success; Aunt Meg had had a long-cherished dream fulfilled and they had seen as much as possible of the city. It would have been nice to go inside some of the magnificent houses they had inspected so avidly from the

streets. It was a pity she hadn't had the wit to do as
Janey suggested; if she had fainted, or appeared to
faint, she would have had to spend much more time
inside Mr van Houben's house and had a chance to
look around. As it was she had barely glimpsed the
hall before the brief session in his study while he dealt
with the grazes. She would know better next time—
only there wouldn't be a next time. She and her aunt
had saved for some time for their holiday; there
wouldn't be one next year, and if there was enough
money for the year following that Aunt Meg would
want to go somewhere else. When holidays were few
and far between one couldn't afford to go to the same
place twice, not if one wanted to see as much of foreign parts as possible.

Impatient with herself for feeling discontented, she
went away to wash her hair and by the time it was
dry and fastened neatly once more it was time for
supper. Afterwards, everyone lucky enough to be off
duty crowded into the sitting-room to drink tea, talk
shop and compare notes about their boyfriends. There
was the usual hospital gossip too: who was going out
with which house doctor, Mr Wilkins' nasty fit of
temper in Theatre that afternoon, Casualty Sister's unjust treatment of one of their number who had had
the misfortune to drop a pile full of sterile dishes...
By the time she got to bed she had forgotten her dis-
content. Life, she thought sleepily, was really quite
fun, and somewhere, some time, she would meet the

man she would marry. He had until now been a nebulous figure, vague as to feature and voice, but now he bore a striking resemblance to Mr van Houben. 'Which really won't do at all,' muttered Caroline as she closed her eyes.

Life was by no means fun the next day. Mr Wilkins' morning round was far from smooth; he had come on to the ward in a bad temper to start with, which rendered the already nervous students even more nervous so that they were either struck dumb or gave all the wrong answers; moreover, several of the ladies lying in their beds dozing peacefully deeply resented being wakened so that he might examine them. Sister Cowie, who prided herself upon the perfection of her ward, pursed her lips and said very little; later several people would get the sharp edge of her tongue. Certainly her nurses would be held to blame for allowing the patients to drop off when Mr Wilkins' round was imminent. Those who could kept prudently out of sight, but Staff Nurse and Corinna, following in Sister's footsteps bearing charts, X-ray forms and all the impedimenta needed to keep Mr Wilkins happy, were very aware of her displeasure. Staff would get the blame, of course, which she would pass on to everyone else.

Two more patients and the round would be finished and Mr Wilkins and his registrar would drink coffee with Sister. He was approaching the last bed when he was nudged aside, his foot trodden on and urged to wait a moment. Caroline, bearing a bowl, reached the patient in the nick of time. An arm around the heaving shoulders, the bowl nicely in position, and sitting on the bed because it was easier, Caroline turned a cheerful face to Mr Wilkins. 'So sorry if I hurt your foot, sir, but Mrs Clarke is always sick without warning—so awkward and horrid for her.'

Mr Wilkins gobbled wordlessly; he was a pompous man, short and stout and middle-aged. He was a splendid surgeon and the students held him in awe, something he rather enjoyed, and here was a dab of a girl actually pushing him aside, telling him to wait. The fact that if he hadn't waited the consequences would have been unpleasant to himself cut no ice. He opened his mouth to administer a dignified rebuke, but Caroline spoke first. 'There—Mrs Clarke is better now.' She mopped the lady's pallid brow and picked up the bowl. 'I do hope,' she added in a motherly voice, 'that your foot isn't painful, sir.'

She slipped away and Sister, Staff and Corinna, who had been holding their breath, let it out with a sigh of relief. Mr Wilkins looked around him but the various faces looking back at him seemed solemn. 'We will now examine Mrs Clarke,' he told them and embarked on a rather lengthy dissertation concerning that lady's insides, very much to her discomfort.

Drinking his coffee presently, Mr Wilkins voiced his disapproval of Caroline's conduct. 'I have neither the time nor the inclination to speak to this nurse,' he observed, 'I rely upon you, Sister, to deal with her as you think fit. I intend to speak to the senior nursing officer, of course. I cannot have my authority undermined.'

Sister, a strict disciplinarian but always fair, spoke up. 'Nurse acted with foresight, sir. If she hadn't reached Mrs Clarke with the bowl you would have been—er...' She paused delicately.

'She pushed me,' said Mr Wilkins crossly, 'and trod on my foot, and then had the impudence to hope that she hadn't hurt me.'

His registrar said quite quietly, 'It was either that or vomit all over your suit, sir. I agree with Sister—Nurse acted promptly in the best interests of both you and your patient.' He added, 'It would be most unjust to blame her for what she obviously saw as her duty.'

Mr Wilkins had gone red. 'Since I am to be outnumbered I shall overlook the matter, but rest assured that I shall make it my business to keep a strict eye on the girl. What is her name?'

'Nurse Frisby. She has just entered her second year. She is a promising student.'

Mr Wilkins said, 'Pish,' and went away, his registrar, poker-faced, with him. He didn't like his chief overmuch, and he was glad that Caroline had escaped his bad temper. He grinned at the thought of the medical students recounting the episode to their fellows. Most of them had suffered at some time from Mr

Wilkins' ill humour and would relish a good laugh at his expense.

All the same, something would have to be done about it, Sister decided, and took herself off to the office to see her superior.

Two days later, before Mr Wilkins' next ward round, Caroline was transferred to the children's ward.

It was a happy choice made by her two superiors. The paediatric unit was housed at the back of the hospital, a modern wing built on to the ponderous Victorian main hospital. It was presided over by an elderly woman, Sister Crump, reputedly as mad as a hatter but none the less a miracle-worker when it came to getting her little patients well again and, what was more important, keeping them happy in the process.

After the strict regime of Women's Surgical, Caroline found it very much to her liking. Here there were no orderly rows of cots; they were wheeled here, there and everywhere according to Sister Crump's mood, and down the centre of the long ward there were low tables cluttered up with toys, teddy bears and picture books and the children who were well enough were allowed to scamper around within reason. On first sight it appeared to be a madhouse, but there was order too, and if a nurse couldn't fit into Sister Crump's way of working she was moved to another ward, for she demanded meticulous care of the children in her charge. Dressings were done, little patients got ready for Theatre, temperatures taken, medicines given to the strains of cheerful music. Since the children, unless they were very ill, shouted and screamed a good deal, the nurses had to lift their voices above the din. There was discipline too: the children addressed all the nurses as Nurse—Christian names, according to Sister Crump, carried no authority with them, and authority, gentle though it might be, was needed at all times.

Sister Crump had liked Caroline at once; nothing to look at, as she observed to Staff Nurse Neville later, but from all accounts she had acted with commendable promptness on the surgical ward even if she had upset Mr Wilkins' sense of importance. 'A fuss about nothing,' she declared, and sailed into the ward, to clap her hands and tell the children to shout more softly. At the same time she observed that Caroline was sitting on the edge of a small bed, holding a little wriggling girl on her lap while a senior nurse dressed the wound, beautifully stitched, on the small arm.

There were side-wards leading from the main wards where the very ill children lay. It was quiet here, the rooms with glass walls, equipped with all the paraphernalia necessary for urgent treatment and nurses constantly going from one child to the other. In a few days, Staff Nurse had told Caroline, when she had got to know the ward thoroughly, she would take her turn too with the other nurses, looking after one or two children, giving them the specialised treatment they had been ordered. Caroline looked at the array of monitoring screens, tubes and drips and hoped that she would know what to do. Of course, Sister Tutor had explained it all, but applying theory to practice demanded the keeping of one's wits about one.

She got on well with the other nurses—they were all her senior but she was a little older than most student nurses and made no effort to call attention to herself; besides, she was willing to help out on occasion and made no demands about having days off to suit herself and not the ward. By the end of the week she had been accepted by both nurses and children alike; moreover, Sister Crump had taken care to introduce her to the various housemen who visited the ward, cheerful young men who were quite willing to waste ten minutes playing with the children, eyeing the nurses and coaxing mugs of coffee out of Sister Crump. And when the consultant paediatrician came to do his round she wasn't exactly introduced, although she was pointed out to him as being the new nurse on the ward. He stared at her, gave her a nod and took no more notice of her; indeed, it would have surprised her very much if he had. He was a youngish man with a long, thin face which lit up when he was with the children. One of the other student nurses, standing discreetly in the background while he went from one small patient to the other, whispered that he

had three small children of his own and had married
a nurse from the hospital. 'The children love him,'
she added, 'and he and old Crumpie get on like a
house on fire.'

Certainly the round had none of the formality of a
grown-ups' ward. Mr Spence sat on the cots and small
beds, carrying, from time to time, a grizzling infant
over a shoulder while he discussed something with
his registrar and the housemen. Caroline went home
for her next days off happier than she had been for
some time, although she had to admit to herself that
if only she could banish Mr van Houben from her
mind she would be completely happy; he was taking
up too much of her thoughts, which was absurd; she
had exchanged only a few words with him and none
of those exciting enough to engage his attention, and
besides, she had made a fool of herself falling down
his steps. If he ever thought of her at all, which she
doubted, it would be with an amused laugh.

When she went back on duty after her days off it
was to be told by Sister Crump that they were short-
handed, what with days off and one of the third-year
students off sick and a badly injured child brought in
late the evening before. 'Ran away from his nanny,
climbed a wall and fell on to a concrete path. Head
injuries and in a coma. Mr Spence doesn't want to
operate until he improves; unfortunately he has broken ribs and a punctured lung, makes giving an anaesthetic very tricky. He's being specialled, Nurse,

which means that for long periods you may be alone in the main ward. Can you manage that?'

'I'll do my best, Sister. There's no one very ill there, is there? It's a question of keeping them happy and potting them and feeding them…'

'Just so. You'll have another nurse with you whenever it's possible and I don't believe that you're a girl to panic. Now, we will go through the charts—there are one or two children you must keep an eye on…'

It wasn't until the afternoon that Caroline was left alone, and it would only be for an hour or so while the other nurse took two children down to the X-ray department. The children had had their after-dinner nap and she had got those who were allowed out of their cots and beds and organised them into manageable groups around the little tables. They were for the most part good; only Bertie, four years old, was a handful. He had been admitted ten days previously, having fallen off a swing in the play-pit below the high-rise flats where his mother lived, twelve storeys high. He hadn't been found for some time and had been taken, concussed and bruised, to the hospital. Sister Crump had spoken severely to his mother about the risk of letting a very small boy play so far out of her sight and she had promised to go to the social worker and get him taken to a pre-school playgroup. In the meanwhile he was enjoying himself enormously, doing everything he shouldn't.

He hadn't settled down with the other children who

were up. Caroline, distributing sheets of paper and coloured pencils, saw him making for the ward doors at the other end and darted after him, to catch him into her arms—just as the doors opened and Mr van Houben walked in.

Caroline, clasping a struggling Bertie to her person, stared up at him, her face alight with surprise and delight. Quite forgetful of where she was, and for that matter who she was, she said happily, 'Oh, hello!'

CHAPTER TWO

CAROLINE saw at once that he wasn't going to remember her. She hoped that he hadn't heard her little burst of speech and asked in her most professional voice, 'Can I help you? Are you looking for someone?'

He looked at her then, but it was impossible to tell if he had recognised her. His handsome face was bland and unsmiling. 'I'm looking for Mr Spence.'

'He's in one of the side-rooms. I think he may be busy. I'm afraid I can't leave the children to tell him that you want to see him.'

She had wasted her breath for he was striding away down the ward and through the archway to the side-rooms. 'Oh, my goodness, I shall get eaten alive,' observed Caroline, a remark which sent Bertie off into a fit of the giggles.

The other nurse had come back presently and they were busy getting the children washed and potted and back into their cots and beds. Caroline was urging the recalcitrant Bertie into his bed when Mr Spence and Mr van Houben came through the ward, walking slowly, deep in talk and followed by Sister and the registrar and two of the housemen. Bertie's loud,

'Hey, Doc,' brought them to a momentary pause, but only long enough to give them time to reply, and that in a rather absent-minded manner. Obviously they had grave matters on their learned minds.

It was Staff Nurse who told her later that the child in the side-room was to be operated on that evening. 'That's why Mr van Houben came—he's a wizard with anaesthetics.' Caroline, all ears, would have liked to have known more, but Staff was busy and presently she went off duty, to change into outdoor clothes and go with various friends to the local cinema.

The ward was its usual bustling, noisy self when she went on duty in the morning; she helped with the breakfasts and then with the rest of the day staff who could be spared, went to Sister's office for the report.

It had been a good night in the main ward; duties were meted out in Sister Crump's fashion, apparently haphazard but adding up to a sensible whole. 'Little Marc in the side room—he'll be specialled of course—usual observations and I'm to be told at once if there's anything you aren't too happy about. Nurse Frisby, you will stay with him until you are relieved at noon. Either Staff Nurse or myself will be checking at regular intervals. The operation was successful—a craniotomy and decompression of the vault—but there is some diffuse neuronal damage and the added complication of a punctured lung. The child is gravely ill but we'll pull him through. There is oedema and some haemorrhaging so be especially on the look out for coning.' She added briskly, 'Back to work, Nurses.'

Staff Nurse went with Caroline, who was relieved to see that there wasn't anything complicated she couldn't understand. The various scans, machines, tubes and charts she had already worked with on Women's Surgical. It was a sharp eye and common sense that was needed, said Staff encouragingly. The child was in a deep coma; all Caroline had to do was to check pulse, breathing and temperature at the time stated on the chart, note any change and let her or Sister know at once. 'Just keep your hand on the panic bell', she was advised, 'and keep your head.' She looked at her watch. 'It's time for observations, so I'll leave you to get on with it.' She cast an eye over the small boy in the bed, his head swathed in bandages, his person attached to various tubes. 'Someone will bring you some coffee,' she added kindly as she went.

Caroline did everything that was necessary, examined the little white face anxiously and took the chair by the bed. The nurse she had relieved had written 'No change' on the chart and with one eye on the child she read the notes on his board. Mr Spence had written a great deal and it took her some time to decipher his writing. Mr van Houben had written a whole lot too. It took her even longer to read, since his writing was so illegible that it could have been in Greek or Sanskrit.

She had just finished her second round of observations when Mr Spence and Mr van Houben came in. They both wished her good morning as she got to her feet and handed over the chart. As she did so, she realised something which she had known subconsciously when she had first studied the chart. Marc's surname was van Houben. Mr van Houben's son? If it were so, where was his mother? She had her answer quicker than she had expected.

'Marc's mother will be here shortly,' said Mr van Houben. 'She will stay only briefly—remain with Marc while she is here. She is likely to be upset.' He smiled briefly from a grim face and turned to Mr Spence. 'Would it be a good idea if…?' He launched into technicalities and Caroline sat down again to keep watch. They thanked her as they went away. It invariably surprised her that the senior men were always civil—with the exception of Mr Wilkins—whereas some of the housemen tended to throw their weight around, wanting this and that and the other thing on the wards, leaving messes to be cleared up.

She was relieved at noon and there was no sign of Marc's mother. She was sent to first dinner and over the cottage pie and spring cabbage she regaled her friends at the table with her morning's work.

'At least it gave your feet a rest,' said someone.

'Yes, but I was so afraid something awful might

happen—he's been unconscious ever since he hurt himself and the operation took hours.'

She bolted rhubarb and custard, drank a cup of tea far too hot and went back on the ward. It was time for the children to have their afternoon rest. Sister had gone to lunch, taking all but the nurse specialling Marc with her, leaving Staff and Caroline to the task of seeing the children who were up and enticing them into their beds and then going around making comfortable those who were bedridden.

'Marc's mother came,' said Staff. 'Mr van Houben came with her, of course.'

Caroline said, 'She must be terribly upset.'

'She was—she's expecting a baby in a week's time. She came over from Holland. She's beautiful—you know—fair hair and blue eyes and the most gorgeous clothes.'

Caroline didn't want to hear about her—of course she would be beautiful, Mr van Houben wouldn't have married a girl less than perfection. 'Is Marc the only one? Other than the baby?'

She lifted out a small sleepy toddler while Staff put in a clean sheet.

'Yes. Mr Spence seems to think that Marc will live but the thing is if he's going to come out of this coma. He may have to operate again.'

'Oh, the poor little boy.' She kissed the top of the baby's head; he had a cleft palate and a hare lip but

Mr Spence would see to those in a day or two. She put him gently back into his cot and tucked him in.

Staff said, 'You like kids, don't you?'

Caroline was at the next cot, changing a nappy. 'Yes.'

Staff was feeling chatty. 'Sister says you're a natural—I dare say you'll end up with a ward full of children and make it your life's work.'

'Yes,' said Caroline again. She did like children, but she would prefer to have her own; vague thoughts of a charming house in the country with dogs and cats and a donkey and, of course, children filled her mind. She would need a husband, of course. Mr van Houben's rather frosty features swam before her eyes and she said, 'Oh, dear, that won't do at all,' so that Staff looked at her and observed kindly,

'Well, there's always the chance that you'll marry.'

She was to special little Marc each morning for the foreseeable future. Sister rambled on rather about his subconscious getting used to the same person by his bedside, so that the three of them shared the twenty-four hours between them. It was towards the end of her eight-hour stint that Mr van Houben came again, and this time with Marc's mother.

Staff hadn't exaggerated. Marc's mother was lovely despite the fact that she was desperately worried and pale with anxiety. She stood by the little bed, staring down at the small face, and Mr van Houben put an arm round her shoulders.

Mr Spence came in then and the two men conferred quietly and Caroline said, 'Sit down for a minute and hold his hand…'

His mother lifted unhappy blue eyes to hers. 'He does not know?'

'Well, we don't know, do we?! I hold it all the time unless I'm doing things for him.'

His mother smiled then. 'You're very nice,' she said, and they sat silently until the men had finished their talk, checked the charts and the three of them had gone away. Caroline sat down again and picked up the limp little paw and held it firmly. It was a way of communication—that was, if communication was possible.

Several days went by and each morning Mr van Houben and Marc's mother came to see him until one morning Mr van Houben arrived early by himself. His, 'Good morning, Nurse,' was curt and he looked as if he had been up all night. If she had known him better she would have told him to go home to bed.

'Well, Marc has a little sister.' He stared down at the inert little figure in the bed and Caroline said, 'Oh, you must be delighted. Congratulations, sir.'

He turned his head to look at her. He looked as though he was going to speak but he only smiled slightly, made sure that Marc's condition was unchanged and went away. He came back with Mr Spence just as she had handed over to her relief, but since there was no reason for her to remain she went away to eat a late lunch in the empty canteen. The boiled cod and white sauce, boiled potatoes and carrots, edible in company and when freshly cooked, had rather lost their appeal. She ate the apple crumble which followed, coaxed a pot of tea from the impatient girl behind the counter and then went to her room and changed into outdoor things—she was off duty until five o'clock and a brisk walk would do her good. She took a bus to Victoria Park and marched along its paths, in no mood to admire the first of the spring flowers braving the chilly day. She had no idea why she was feeling so edgy; perhaps she was hungry or just a little homesick for Aunt Meg's cosy little house—or was she just anxious about Marc, who was making no progress at all. Walking back presently to catch her bus back to the hospital, she admitted to herself that it wasn't any of these things—it was Mr van Houben's smile when she had congratulated him. It had been faintly mocking, slightly amused, as though she had made a bad joke. Sitting squashed between two stout women with bulging shopping bags, Caroline told herself to stop thinking about him, that there was no point in doing so, and when presently, as she was crossing the forecourt to the hospital entrance, he went past her, on his way to the consultant's car park, she glared at him so ferociously that he paused and turned to look at her small person; even from the back she looked cross.

When she went back on duty it was to be told that

it was intended to operate on Marc again. 'Seven o'clock, Nurse,' said Sister Crump. 'You'll probably have to stay on duty; Mr Spence wants two of you specialling for the first twelve hours. You'll stay until a second nurse can come on around midnight. That'll be Staff or myself.'

She nodded, her cap slightly askew. 'You and Nurse Foster get Marc ready for Theatre—she's off duty at six o'clock, and you'll take him to Theatre. Understood?' She smiled at Caroline. 'Run along. We'll have to fit in your supper somewhere, but at the moment I don't know when.'

Marc would be wheeled to Theatre on his little bed; they did everything needed, checked the equipment, did their observations, and when Nurse Foster went off duty Caroline sat down to wait, holding Marc's small hand in hers. She liked Theatre work, although she didn't know much about it; she had done a short stint during her first year but it hadn't been enough for her to learn much beyond the care of instruments, the filling of bowls and the conveying of nameless objects in kidney dishes to and from the path lab. She hoped now that she wouldn't have to go into Theatre; she had grown attached to the silent small boy, away in some remote world of his own, and the thought of Mr Spence standing with scalpel at the ready made her feel a little sick.

Mr van Houben was in the anaesthetic room, some-how managing to look distinguished in his Theatre

kit—a loose pale blue smock and trousers topped by
a cap which would have done very nicely to have
covered a steamed pudding. He was joined by Mr
Spence and then by his registrar and all three men
held a muttered conversation while Caroline stood patiently by the bed, admiring the back of Mr van
Houben's head, never mind the cap.

It was a disappointment to her that presently one
of the staff nurses from Theatre took her place and
she was dismissed with a laconic, 'Thanks, Nurse.'

. She went back to the ward and made up the bed
and checked the equipment and was then sent to her
supper. 'They'll send down one of the ITC nurses,'
Sister Crump told her, 'but you'd better be there to
fetch and carry.'

The day staff were going off duty when Caroline
went back; the children were sleeping as Sister Crump
did a round with the night nurses, and paused to speak
to Caroline as she went. 'I'll be back presently,' she
told her.

It was after ten o'clock when Marc came back to
his little room. Once he was again in his own bed, it
was just a question of his being linked up with the
apparatus around him and a careful check made as to
his condition. Sister Crump had appeared silently to
see things for herself and presently Mr Spence and
Mr van Houben came in. The little room was full of
people, and Caroline, feeling unnecessary, tucked herself away in a corner. Sister Crump caught her eye

presently. 'Go off duty, Nurse,' she said briskly.
'Come on at ten o'clock tomorrow.'

Caroline went, feeling anxious about little Marc
and rather put out since her off duty had been
changed—and she had agreed to go to the pictures on
the following evening with Janey and several other of
her friends.

She yawned her way into a bath and, despite her
concern for the little boy, went to sleep at once.

Marc was still there when she went on duty in the
morning; she had been half afraid that he wouldn't
have survived the night but there he lay, looking just
as before, with Mr van Houben checking the tangle
of tubes around the bed, calculating the drip and then
taking a sample of blood from the small hand lying
so still on the very white coverlet. He turned to look
at Caroline as she went in. 'Ask Sister Crump to come
here, will you, Nurse? You're taking over here?'

'Yes, sir.' She sped away to fetch Sister Crump and
then con the charts with the nurse she was to relieve.
He had looked at her, she thought sadly, as though
he had never seen her before.

It was two days later, halfway through the morning,
that Marc's hand, lying in Caroline's, curled gently
over. For a moment she couldn't believe it and then
she wanted to shout for someone to come, press the
panic bell, do a dance for joy… Her training took
over; she sat quietly and waited and sure enough
within a minute or so his hand turned again, a grace-

ful languid movement as though it were returning to life. Which of course it was.

She did press the panic bell then. Sister Crump got there first.

'He moved his hand in mine—twice,' said Caroline.

'The good Lord be thanked,' said Sister Crump. The two other nurses had arrived. 'One of you ring Mr Spence or his registrar—one or other is to come at once. The other nurse to go back to the ward.'

The nurses went and Caroline said softly, 'Look, Sister.'

The small hand was moving again, curling round her thumb.

Mr Spence had just finished his list in Theatre and he still wore his Theatre kit as he came soft-footed to stand by the bed, followed by his registrar.

'Give your report, Nurse,' said Sister Crump.

Which Caroline did, trying to keep the quiver of excitement out of her voice. Put into a few sparse words it didn't sound much, but as she spoke Marc lifted his arm very slightly as though he wanted to make himself more comfortable. 'Eureka,' said Mr Spence softly. 'Someone get hold of Mr van Houben.'

He wasn't in the hospital, although he had left a phone number where he could be reached. It was two or three hours later by the time he entered the room, looking calm and unflustered, giving no indication that he had been driving hell-for-leather down the M1

from Birmingham where he had gone to give his
opinion concerning the anaesthetising of a patient
with a collapsed lung and a tracheotomy into the bargain.

It was at that moment that Marc opened his eyes,
blinked and closed them again.

'Too soon to carry out any tests,' said Mr Spence.
'Another three or four hours—do you agree?' When
Mr van Houben nodded, he added, 'We'll be back
around four o'clock, Sister.' His eye lighted on
Caroline, sitting like a small statue, not moving. 'You
are to stay with Marc, Nurse.'

Which made sense; she had seen the very first
movements, and she was in a better position to gauge
his progress or deterioration than anyone else coming
fresh to the scene. All the same, she hoped that someone would bring her a cup of coffee before Mr Spence
returned.

They did better than that. A tray of tea and sandwiches was brought and arranged where she could get
at it without disturbing the child, and, besides, Sister
Crump was in and out every hour or so. Marc hadn't
moved again; Caroline had charted his movements
carefully, noting with delight that his temperature had
come down a little. Certainly his pulse was steady.

She was stiff and cramped by the time the men
came back. Mr Spence said, 'Good—take over, Sister,
will you?' And watched while Caroline withdrew her
hand, only to have it clutched again.

'You'd better stay; we don't want him disturbed in any way.'

A silly remark, thought Caroline, watching the gentle poking and prodding, the tickling of the small feet with a pin, the meticulous examination for pupil reaction, for Marc was disturbed, making small fretful movements and wriggling at the touch of a pin. But of course that was what they had hoped for: all the signs of a return to consciousness. The three men and Sister Crump bent over the bed and Caroline sat on a hard chair out of their way. She was happy about little Marc; it was the nicest thing which had happened to her for a long time. Mr van Houben must be over the moon, she reflected, although it was too early to tell if there would be lasting damage to little Marc; he had a long way to go still... Feeling selfish and uncaring, she longed for a cup of tea. At such dramatic moments cups of tea and feeling tired were not to be considered.

Little Marc had fallen asleep again—natural sleep now, not a coma—and the men were still discussing further treatment. It was Sister Crump, her eyes lighting upon Caroline's small person in a corner, who exclaimed, 'Go off duty, Nurse, I'm sorry you're late. You've missed your tea—go to the canteen and see if they'll boil you an egg or let you have your supper early. You missed your lunch?'

Caroline nodded and stood up. The men were writing now, absorbed in their problems. She whispered,

'Good evening, Sister,' and slipped out of the room and down the ward and out on to the landing beyond before anyone had a chance to say anything to her. Presumably the nurse to relieve her was already waiting; Sister Crump would be there to brief her. She made her way down to the canteen and found no one there, something she had half expected, for tea had been finished hours ago and first supper wasn't until seven o'clock. All the same she went up to the counter in case there was someone beyond it in the serving-room.

'No good your coming in here, Nurse. You know as well as I do that there's nothing to be had between meals. Supper's at the usual time; you'll just have to wait.'

So calmly Caroline went away again, back up the stairs to the ground floor; she would make a pot of tea and take off her shoes and sit and drink it and then, tired though she was, get into a coat and go for a brisk walk. The streets round the hospital were shabby and houses down at heel, but it had been a grey April day and dusk cast a kindly mantle over them. She didn't much care for a walk in such surroundings, but fresh air and exercise seemed more important than any other consideration.

She started along the corridor which ran at the back of the entrance hall and then stopped with a small gasp when she was tapped on the shoulder.

Mr van Houben, unhurried and as always, immaculate, was at her side. 'When did you go on duty, Nurse?'

'Ten o'clock, sir.'

'You have had no off duty?'

'I'm off now,' she told him and added, 'sir' as she started off again.

'Not so fast. Did I hear Sister Crump say that you have had no proper meal today?'

'I have had sandwiches and coffee…' She stopped to think—it seemed a long time ago.

'Yes, yes—I said a meal.'

'I shall go to supper presently.'

'You deserve better than that. I'm hungry too; we'll go and find somewhere to eat.'

'We'll what?' She goggled at the sight of him, her mouth open like a surprised child. 'But you can't do that…'

'Why not?' he asked coolly. 'I am not aware that I am restricted in my actions by anyone or anything.'

'Well, no, of course you're not. I mean, you don't have to bother, do you? But it really wouldn't do, you know. Important people like you don't take junior nurses out to dinner.'

'You are mistaken, we aren't going to dinner. Go and put on a coat and some powder on your nose and we will go to the Bristling Dog down the street and eat sausages out of a basket.'

He didn't wait for her reply. 'And comb your hair,' he advised her kindly as he gave her a gentle shove in the direction of the door to the nurses' home. He added, 'If you aren't back here within ten minutes I shall come and find you.'

'You can't...' He must be light-headed with hunger, she decided, or in a state of euphoria because Marc had shown the first tentative signs of recovery.

He said coldly, 'Can I not?' and gave her a steely look which sent her through the door and up the stairs to her room.

He had said ten minutes and he had undoubtedly meant what he had said. Caroline had never changed so fast in her life before. She raced out of her room and almost fell over Janey.

'Hey—where are you off to?' Janey made a grasp at her arm.

'I can't stop,' said Caroline breathlessly, 'he said in ten minutes...'

She raced down the stairs and Janey, five minutes later, told those of her friends who were in the sitting-room that Caroline had gone out with a man.

'Good for her,' said someone. 'It's time she had some fun.'

If Caroline had heard that remark she would have felt doubtful about the fun. Mr van Houben was waiting for her, looking remote, almost forbidding, and she very nearly turned tail and went back through the door. The prospect of a good supper was a powerful incentive, however, and she went to where he was standing and said quietly, 'Well, here I am, Mr van Houben.'

He stood for a moment looking down at her. She had got into the first thing which had come to hand, a short jacket over a thin sweater and a pleated skirt, and, because ten minutes hadn't been nearly long enough, her hair, though tidy, had been pinned back ruthlessly into a bun instead of its usual french pleat, and there had been even less time to spend on her face.

Mr van Houben laughed inwardly at his sudden decision to take this small unassuming person out for a meal. It had been triggered off by the sight of her sitting by little Marc; she had been the one who had first seen his faint stirrings and acted promptly, but no one had so much as spared her a smile and she had been sent off duty without so much as a thank-you. She must have longed to share their triumph and relief. He was a kind man; at least he could make up for that by giving her a meal.

He said with impersonal friendliness, 'You hadn't anything planned for this evening?' As he ushered her through the doors and out into the forecourt.

She answered him in her sensible way, 'No, nothing at all.'

He took her arm as they crossed the busy street. 'No boyfriend to disappoint?' He was sorry he had said that for, looking down at her in the light of a street lamp, he saw the look on her face and to make amends he added, 'I should imagine that there is little time for serious friendships while you are training. Plenty of time for that once that's done with! You might like to travel—there are quite a number of English nurses in our bigger hospitals in Holland.'

He eased the conversation into impersonal channels until they reached the Bristling Dog, where he urged her into the saloon bar, half filled already, mostly by elderly couples and a sprinkling of younger people, most of them eating as well as drinking, and several, Caroline noticed, from the hospital.

Mr van Houben sat her down at a small corner table and fetched the well-thumbed menu card from the bar. It held a surprising variety of food, but Mr van Houben had suggested sausages... 'Sausages and chips, please,' she told him, anxious to fall in with his own wishes.

'Splendid,' he said, and with unerring instinct, 'and a pot of tea?'

He was rewarded with her smile. 'That would be nice.'

The food came, hot and tasty, and with it a pot of tea and thick cups and saucers. Caroline poured out and handed him his cup. It was strong, and even with milk and sugar he found it unpalatable. All the same, he drank a second cup because it was obvious that Caroline expected him to. He was rewarded by her sweet smile and the observation given in matter-of-fact tones that a cup of tea was a splendid pick-me-up when tired.

Over the last of the chips he asked her what she thought of London. 'You live here?' he asked casually.

'No, I live with my aunt at Basing—that's near Basingstoke. I go home twice a month.'

'The English countryside is very charming,' he observed, and from then until they returned to the hospital they talked about it, and the weather, of course, a conversation which gave him no insight as to her likes and dislikes. She was a sensible girl with nice manners and a gentle way with her, and he was surprised to discover that he had rather enjoyed his evening with her. He bade her goodnight in the entrance hall and listened to her nicely put thanks and didn't tell her that he would be returning to Holland in the morning. Marc's father, recalled from a remote region of South America where he was building a bridge, would be installed with his wife and baby daughter by now, and Mr van Houben could return to his own work with a moderately easy mind.

He watched her go through the door at the back of the hall and made his way to the children's wing where he found Mr Spence, his brother Bartus and Sister Crump, who quite often stayed on duty if she saw fit.

'Very satisfactory,' said Mr Spence. 'We're not out

of the wood but there's plenty of movement. You'll be over again?'

Marius van Houben nodded. 'In a few days, just a flying visit.' He put a large hand on his brother's shoulder. 'You'll stay with Emmie until we know how things are? As soon as he's fit, perhaps we could get him back home with a nurse but that's early days yet...'

'A good idea all the same,' agreed Mr Spence. 'Familiar surroundings may be the answer.'

'I'm going along to Theatre to collect up my equipment, I'll give you a lift back, Bartus—see you at the car presently.' He bade Mr Spence goodnight with the remark that he would see him before he left the next day, and with a last look at his small nephew he went away. Sister Crump caught up with him as he reached the end of the ward. It was very quiet, the children slept and the night nurses were sitting in the middle of the ward at the night table, shadowy figures under the dark red lampshade.

'I'm sorry you're going,' said Sister Crump in a whisper. 'Marc wouldn't have pulled through without your expertise.'

She wasn't praising him, just stating a fact. 'I don't like to lose a patient.'

'He has had splendid nursing care.'

'Yes—they're good girls.' She frowned. 'I hope that child had a meal—I should have made sure. She went off duty very late too.'

Mr van Houben smiled down at her worried face. 'She had sausages and chips and a pot of the strongest tea I have ever been forced to drink.'

'You? You were with her?'

'We met in the entrance hall and I happened to be hungry too.' He opened the door, 'Goodnight, Sister.'

Sister Crump went back to Mr Spence. She was smiling widely but she rearranged her features into suitable severity as she joined him.

Caroline was pounced upon by Janey on her way to the bath. 'Where have you been?' demanded her friend. 'And who with? And why were you in such a hurry?'

She had been joined by various of Caroline's friends and one of them added, 'Have you been out to dinner?'

'No—just the Bristling Dog.'

There was a concerted gasp. 'But nurses don't go there. Whoever took you there and why didn't you tell him?'

'Well, I didn't like to—I suppose he can go where he likes and if I was with him it wouldn't matter.'

'Who?' They hissed at her from all sides.

'Mr van Houben.'

One of her listeners was doing her six weeks in Theatre. 'Him? That marvellous man who came specially to give the anaesthetic for Marc? Caroline, how did you do it? We've all had a go at him...'

'He asked me if I was hungry and when I said yes, he said he was too.'

'Oh, love,' said Janey, 'you were wearing that jacket you've had for ages, the one that doesn't fit very well across the shoulders.'

'He told me to be ready in ten minutes or he'd come and fetch me. I hadn't time…'

Her friends groaned. 'What did you eat?'

She told them. 'And a pot of tea.' She thought for a bit. 'And we talked about little Marc and the weather and how flat Holland is…'

'He won't even remember you,' groaned Janey. 'Why didn't you tell him that you would like to go out to a splendid meal at the Savoy or something? He might have taken the hint.'

'I didn't think of anything like that. I mean, I don't really think that anyone would want to take me to the Savoy.' Caroline was quite matter-of-fact about it. 'Least of all someone like him.' She hitched up her dressing-gown. 'I'm on early.'

When she got back to her room there was a note waiting for her telling her to report for duty at ten o'clock instead of half-past seven. A nice surprise, and she switched off her alarm clock and went quite contentedly to sleep.

By the time she arrived on the ward in the morning, Mr van Houben had been to see Marc, bidden good-bye to Sister Crump and left the hospital. He had, for the moment, quite forgotten Caroline.

CHAPTER THREE

LITTLE Marc was restless; Caroline watched with some anxiety as Mr Spence examined him soon after she had taken over from the other nurse. 'A good sign,' he pronounced at length. 'Keep an eye open, Nurse, and try and keep him with us—talk to him…' He glanced at her. 'You always held his hand, didn't you? Quite right too…'

He went away and she was left alone with the little boy and her charts. Presently he began to fidget again, although he quietened when she began to talk to him and then sing. She chose, 'Sing a song of sixpence' and sang it in a rather small clear voice. She went through all the verses several times and was rewarded by his sudden reluctant smile and, even better, a fleeting look from his eyes. She had embarked on the song again when Sister Crump came in and he opened his eyes again.

Mr Spence, called by a delighted Sister Crump, rumbled his satisfaction. 'Sing, did you?' he asked Caroline. 'Be good enough to sing again and let us see what happens.'

She went through the first verse of the rhyme again and Marc opened his eyes once more and this time said something which sounded very much like six-pence before dropping off into a refreshing sleep.

'Well, well,' said Mr Spence, 'bar accidents, I do believe we're out of the wood.'

She was preparing to hand over to the relieving nurse when Marc's mother arrived, accompanied by a thick-set man with a good-looking, rugged face and Sister Crump. She was quite beautiful, only a little pale. She gave Caroline a quick smile and went to the bedside. 'He is better?' she asked softly.

'Coming along nicely,' said Sister Crump gruffly. 'Responded to Nurse singing to him, spoke—only one word, but he spoke.'

The man had his arm round Marc's mother and they stood together looking down at the sleeping boy. Then she asked, 'You are the nurse who has been so watchful and kind; my brother-in-law tells me this.'

She had come to stand by Caroline, smiling a little.

'Your brother-in-law?' Caroline shot a look at the man still by the bed.

'That is my husband—my brother-in-law—the anaesthetist, Marc's uncle...'

'Oh—oh, I see. I thought he was Marc's father.'

'No, no. My husband was in South America, so far away he could not come at once, you understand, and I also...Marius came at once. So lucky he is devoted to Marc. Now my husband is here with me, Marius was able to go back to Holland where he is much occupied in many hospitals.'

She turned to Sister Crump. 'We may stay?' she asked. 'If we are very quiet and do not speak.'

'Of course you may stay,' Sister Crump was brisk, 'and talk to him, take a chair by the bed and hold his hand and talk—sing too, if you like. His father can sit on the other side of the bed. He is going up and down through layers of consciousness and it is very likely that when he is only lightly unconscious he will know you are here.' She frowned. 'Do you understand me? It's difficult to explain.'

'I understand you well, sister, and we will do as you say.' She turned to Caroline. 'And we shall see you again, yes?'

'No, I'm going off duty now, but Nurse Foster is here in my place—we take it in turns. I hope he opens his eyes while you are here.' She smiled widely. 'You could tell him about his baby sister...'

'Yes, yes, we will. She is so beautiful—he will love her.'

Caroline handed over to Nurse Foster, bade everyone there a good afternoon and went off duty.

She loitered along the corridors, thinking about Mr van Houben. She was filled with a pleasure she didn't quite understand because he wasn't married after all, but this was rather damped down by the knowledge that he could have told her that but hadn't chosen to do so. There was no reason why he should, she told herself reasonably as she climbed the stairs to her room, and since she would certainly not see him again, or, if she did, briefly if he came to visit his nephew, there was no point in pursuing the matter further. She had a shower, changed into her outdoor things and caught a bus to Oxford Street to look at the shops. She was to go on duty at seven o'clock the next morning and then, that same evening, go on night duty to special Marc. She quite looked forward to night duty but it did mean that a brisk walk before bed was the only excitement she would have. Of course there would be nights off and she would go home to Basing for three days. It was a cheering thought.

She was off duty again by midday next day, and went to have her dinner and retire to her room to doze until the early evening, when it was presumed that she would get up, dress and present herself at night nurses' breakfast, served at half-past six in the evening. Officially this was what everyone did, although in reality the afternoon rest was cut short and tea was drunk with whoever happened to be off duty too.

Caroline filled in the afternoon with writing a few letters, phoning her aunt and washing her hair before joining such of her friends as were off duty for tea, and then getting back into her uniform and going to the canteen.

Marc was asleep when she took the report from the nurse she was relieving. He had had a good day; his moments of wakefulness were getting more frequent and he had opened his blue eyes and looked at his mother. In the early hours of the morning he woke, and started to talk, normal childish chatter as far as she could judge, and, since there was nothing else to do about it, she answered him in English, and presently, apparently altogether satisfied with what she had said, he went back to sleep.

'Very hopeful,' observed Mr Spence, coming to see how he was a short time before she went off duty. 'A pity you don't speak Dutch. Let us hope that he is wakeful when his mother comes later on today.'

Caroline, by now tired and sleepy, gave him an owlish look. She longed for her bed and the very idea of speaking any other language than basic English at the moment filled her with unease. She gathered her wits together, gave a succinct report to Sister Crump and the nurse taking over and went down to her supper. Topsy-turvy meals took a day or two to get used to; she drank a great many cups of tea, dozed peacefully in the bath and climbed into bed, to sleep all day.

Marc improved by the day, and at the end of her fourth night of duty, with welcome nights off within her grasp, she surveyed his small sleeping person with deep satisfaction. He was sleeping naturally now and having quite long periods of consciousness. She still sang to him, for he seemed to like that, and when he had something to say she answered him in a soothing voice, and when he smiled she smiled too. They had established a rapport which took no heed of the language barrier.

Mr van Houben came just after six o'clock in the morning, faultlessly turned out, his linen spotless, looking as though he had risen from a long, refreshing sleep.

Caroline's heart gave a pleased lurch at the sight of him and instantly it was overshadowed by the knowledge that her own face needed urgent attention and that her hair had escaped the smooth coils she had pinned back so ruthlessly. It was all very well for him, she thought, suddenly peevish, he'd had a splendid night in bed…

Mr van Houben, who had caught a late-night ferry and driven himself to London during the very early hours of the morning, read her thoughts accurately and smiled. His 'good morning' was brisk and he went at once to look at his small nephew.

'Marc,' he said softly, and the little boy opened his eyes and chuckled. His uncle sat down on the edge of the bed and she listened to his quiet voice and after a moment to Marc's hesitant answers. They were interrupted by Night Sister who, Caroline saw with envy, had found time to put on more lipstick and powder her nose. She was a handsome young woman and she gave him an intelligent report using, Caroline noted even more peevishly, Caroline's own carefully written account of the night.

Mr van Houben listened with courteous attention,

his eyes on Sister's face and at the same time aware of Caroline's feelings. Very prickly, he reflected; probably tired. He still felt vaguely guilty about her, although he had no reason to be so. He would ask to see Corinna before he left the hospital and see if there was something to be done to show Marc's parents' appreciation. Tickets for the theatre, he thought vaguely and thanked Sister nicely for her excellent report.

He went away with her, nodding to Caroline and giving her a smile. 'I wish he hadn't come,' she whispered to Marc, who smiled widely and went back to sleep.

Corinna, called from her breakfast to speak to her cousin, flung herself at him. 'Darling Marius, how nice to see you. Are you here for days or just a quick visit? Isn't it wonderful about Marc? I spent my days off with Emmie and Bartus and the baby—she's gorgeous. Do hurry up and get married so that I can be an aunt. Are you going there now?'

'Yes. Tell me, Corinna, that girl who delivered the book—Caroline? She's been looking after Marc?'

'She's one of three—they do eight-hour shifts round the clock. But she gets marvellous reactions from him; I think he likes her very much—well, she's a nice person, you know.' She glanced at him. 'Have you seen her? She's been on night duty—got nights off this morning, though. I saw her yesterday when I went to see Marc; she's going home.' She glanced at him enquiringly. 'Did you want to see her?'

His 'no' was casual. 'I'm only over for a couple of days; I've a consultation in the morning. If you're free this evening I'll take you out to dinner?'

'Lovely, I can be ready by half-past seven, but don't you want to see Emmie?'

'I'll go there for lunch.'

She leaned up and kissed his cheek. 'You're really rather a nice cousin,' she told him, 'Now I must fly— I'm late.'

She blew him a kiss and raced away and he went through the hospital, had a word with the head porter and went out to his car. The street beyond the forecourt was teeming with traffic and the pavements jammed with people hurrying to work. He carefully eased the car into the westbound traffic and waited patiently behind a bus stop while the queue slowly dwindled. The last person in it was Caroline, a small holdall clutched in one hand. He opened the car door and leaned across. 'Caroline, get in,' and even while he was saying it he wondered what had possessed him to do it.

She hesitated and the bus conductor growled, 'Make up yer mind, lady,' pinged the bell and the bus drew away from the curb.

'Get in, do,' said Mr van Houben urgently, impervious to the car behind him, whose driver was leaning on the horn. 'And look sharp about it.'

Caroline, who had no intention of doing any such thing, felt that circumstances were beyond her control. She got in and was barely seated before he drove on. 'I've missed my bus,' she told him tartly. 'Be good enough to put me down at the next bus stop or I shall miss my train.'

'I'm going your way; I'll give you a lift, since I'm the cause of your missing your train.' He spoke carelessly, without a word of truth. He was on the way to his house in the quiet corner of Chiswick where his sister-in-law was staying, and he wished that he hadn't given way to a sudden impulse to give Caroline a lift: heaven knew his day was full enough without the added chore of driving to some small village he had never heard of, yet he had said that he was going her way. He searched his excellent memory for the name of the place and remembered it. 'You'll have to direct me when we get near Basingstoke,' he told her. 'It's close by, I believe.'

He glanced at her; she was looking straight ahead; her profile looked disapproving, her tip-tilted nose in the air, her chin lifted. He couldn't see her eyes, only the curling sweep of their lashes.

'You need to turn off at the roundabout, on to the A30, then there's a small road to Basing.'

He drove out of London and on to the motorway, driving fast and making desultory conversation from time to time. At least they had something in common—the recovery of little Marc. He found that he was enjoying talking about the child, for she was an intelligent listener, but presently they lapsed into silence until they reached the roundabout and turned off the motorway.

'The turning is on the right,' said Caroline once they were on the A30, 'a few miles still. I hope this hasn't taken you out of your way.' She spoke stiffly and then, because she was tired and cross, added, 'It's your own fault if it has; you insisted on giving me a lift.'

Mr van Houben's eyebrows rose a fraction. He was being taken to task for a charitable act which was costing him ill-spared leisure time with his sister.

He sighed and said silkily, 'I see that I have unwittingly annoyed you. How mortifying it is to have what one hoped was a kindly act thrown in one's face. I must bear it in mind in the future.'

An urgent hand came down on his coat sleeve. 'Oh, I'm sorry, I'm sorry, I definitely didn't mean that, truly I didn't. I'm tired and cross but that's no excuse—do please forgive me.'

He glanced down at the small hand in its rather shabby glove and slowed the car to a halt in a lay-by. 'Nothing to forgive,' he told her soothingly. 'I have it on the best authority that you are good tempered, patient and a young woman of sound common sense, all of which virtues have been put severely to the test during the last week or so. Let fly at me if you feel you would like to; it won't bother me in the least.'

She looked away from him out of the window; he was being kind, but what girl would wish to be known for the attributes he had just mentioned? What was the use of any of them if one had a face which Aunt Meg's neighbour had once described as homely? She said quietly. 'It's very kind of you not to mind. I expect I need a day or two away from the hospital.'

Mr van Houben said cheerfully, 'We all need that from time to time, don't we? What do you do when you're at home?'

'Oh, potter in the garden and go out with my aunt.' She searched her mind for something more exciting without success. 'It's just nice being free.'

'The bright lights don't appeal to you?' he asked idly.

A difficult question to answer if by bright lights he meant dinners and dancing and being taken to the theatre. True, she had been to see various shows with such of her friends who, as she had done, had saved up to join the queues for the cheaper seats. Of course there was the annual Hospital Ball, when the consultants danced with each other's wives and the sisters and the housemen picked the prettiest nurses. She had never lacked for partners, for she was much liked, but being liked was quite different from being fallen in love with, and that never happened. She said carefully, 'I don't get a great deal of time to go out and about.'

Mr van Houben thought of his cousin Corinna, who as far as he could make out was burning the candle at both ends and thriving on it. He said kindly, 'No, I don't suppose you do. Is this the turning to Basing?'

The village was red-brick, the small houses each with a garden, and nice little green patches here and there well shaded by trees. There was no one about, no car to be seen or heard, and he stopped the car before Aunt Meg's door...

'Will you come in and have a cup of coffee?' Caroline spoke diffidently.

He had got out to open her door. 'That would be delightful. What a charming village this is. I'm not surprised that you enjoy coming back to it.'

Theobald was sitting in the centre of the little porch, sunning himself, and since it was clear he had no intention of moving they stepped carefully around him and through the half-open door into the narrow little hall. The door at its end led directly onto the back garden and they could see Aunt Meg bending over a flower-bed. She looked up and saw them, dusted her hands off on her apron and came to meet them.

'Nice and early, love,' she told Caroline, kissing her briskly. 'And who is this?'

She held out a hand and smiled up at Mr van

Houben's face. 'Whoever you are, you'll have a cup of coffee, won't you?'

'This is Mr van Houben, Aunt Meg; he kindly gave me a lift as he was coming this way.' She glanced at his impassive face. 'My aunt, Miss Frisby.'

They shook hands and her aunt said cosily, 'Now, isn't that nice? Come in, do—coffee is ready, I was just going to have mine.'

It was a small house, a cottage really, low-ceilinged with a small sitting-room and a larger kitchen leading from it. Mr van Houben, urged to sit down, chose a chair which he hoped would sustain his not inconsiderable weight and looked around him. The room was nicely furnished with some nice pieces, too good for the cottage. Possibly they had been salvaged from a larger house. There were one or two pieces of good silver on the small mahogany side-table too... Caroline had joined him, sitting uneasily on a small Victorian balloon chair, and he began a casual conversation, trying to put her at her ease, sensing that she was shy, although why she should be in her own home was something that he found strange, and nowadays a shy girl was almost unknown.

Aunt Meg came in and he stood up and took the tray from her and put it down on the pedestal table in the centre of the room, taking care not to bang his head on the ceiling beams.

The coffee was hot and delicious and there was a plate of homemade biscuits with it. He sat for twenty minutes or so, talking about nothing much and then listening to Aunt Meg's enthusiastic account of their holiday in Amsterdam, putting in a word here and there, surprised to find someone so knowledgeable about the city and enjoying her views of it.

Presently he turned to Caroline, 'You enjoyed your stay too?' he asked her.

'Oh, yes, very much, only two weeks isn't long enough, is it? But I'm glad we went, and we saw as much as we could, although we missed places—we walked a lot, just looking at all the streets and houses.'

'The best way to see a place,' he said. He put his cup down. 'I must get on—thank you for the coffee and a delightful talk—I hope you will visit Holland again some time.'

He shook hands with Aunt Meg, but he only smiled at Caroline. 'I expect I shall see you at the hospital— I like to keep an eye on young Marcus.'

She went with him to the gate. 'Thank you for bringing me home. I hope it hasn't interfered with your plans.'

He assured her that it hadn't. He sounded impatient, so she didn't believe him. He got into the car and with a casual wave drove away, and she went back indoors, puzzled as to why he had given her a lift—there had been no need, and she was more and more sure by the minute that it hadn't been in his plans for the day.

Which of course it hadn't. He drove himself back to London telling himself that he had repaid Caroline, although it escaped him for the moment why he had to repay her. He dismissed her from his mind and drove to Chiswick to have lunch with his sister-in-law.

The house was in a quiet street, one of a terrace of Georgian villas, all immaculately kept, their front doors with handsome transoms above and splendidly polished brass knockers. Steps led to their doors from the pavement and the street was divided by a narrow strip of tree-shaded grass, iron railings guarding it. Mr van Houben got out of his car and mounted the steps of the end house, inserted the key in the lock and let himself in.

He was met in the hall by a dignified middle-aged man who gave him a faintly disapproving good morning. 'Or should I say good afternoon, sir?'

Mr van Houben shrugged off his coat. 'Yes, well, Breeze, I got held up. Is Mevrouw van Houben here?'

'In the drawing room, sir; Mrs Breeze held back lunch.'

'Splendid—ask her to hold it back about five minutes more while I have a drink, will you?'

He crossed the hall and went into the room at the front of the house and found his sister-in-law sitting by a brisk fire.

'There you are, Marius. Bartus had an appointment

with someone or other and he hopes to be back this afternoon. You're very late.'

'I got held up. How's my niece?'

'Gorgeous.' She took the glass of sherry he had poured for her and smiled a little tremulously. 'Marius, Marc will be all right, won't he? He talks to me now, but every now and then he—he goes away...'

'As he improves he will go away less and less, my dear. You must have patience—a day at a time, and never let him see that you worry about him.'

'I do try—I wish I could be like that funny little nurse with the enormous eyes—she's—I think the word is serene. I have the feeling that when she is with him he feels safe—do you know what I mean?'

'He will need a nurse when you go back to Holland—it will be too much for the nanny you've engaged to cope with the baby and him, and however much you want to be with him you will have to have help.'

They went into the dining-room across the hall, a small room furnished with great good taste in mahogany; lovely old pieces beautifully carved and cared for. Facing him across the oval table, with its lace mats and shining silver and glass, Emmie said, 'But he'll hate having to be looked after by a stranger.'

Mr van Houben picked up this spoon and surveyed the watercress soup Breeze had set before him. 'Yes, I think he will.'

'Then you'll have to do something about it.' She sounded quite fierce.

'Very well,' said Mr van Houben, allowing a vague plan to take shape at the back of his powerful brain. 'I'll see what can be done.'

He wouldn't say any more. They ate their duckling with orange sauce, straw potatoes and baby carrots, followed by feather-light castle puddings, and then sat over their coffee.

'I must say that you live very comfortably,' said Emmie, reverting to Dutch. 'I mean, you've got the house in Amsterdam and Fram and Anna to look after you, and when you come here you've got the Breezes—I must say she's a splendid cook.' She glanced at her brother-in-law across the table. 'Don't you ever want to marry and spend your money on a wife and children?' She saw his quick frown. 'Oh, I know you almost married, but that was years ago. Do you ever think about her?'

He said rather curtly, 'No,' but Emmie persisted.

'I don't suppose you remember what she looks like any more…?'

He gave a reluctant laugh then. 'No, I don't.'

'So there you are. Come and stay with us when you have a few days to spare, Marius, and I'll line up some girls for you to meet.'

'The very idea terrifies me. Shall we go back to the drawing-room? Bartus should be back soon. I'm taking Corinna out to dinner, by the way.'

He had closed the door in her face; they were fond of each other but he had never permitted her to know too much of his private life. They spent the next half-hour talking about nothing in particular, although Emmie returned over and over again to Marc.

'Try not to worry,' her brother-in-law advised her gently. 'I think it's very likely that Marc senses your fears and that isn't going to help him.'

He was sitting opposite her in one of the comfortable armchairs scattered about the room, unshakeably calm. He smiled at her very kindly and she smiled shakily back. 'You're really a very nice man,' she told him. 'I'm going to feed the baby. When Bartus comes, will you both come up and see her?'

Bartus came in very shortly afterwards and the two men sat talking until the maternity nurse who was to stay until Emmie and Bartus went back to Holland came to tell them that *Mevrouw* was waiting for them.

Mr van Houben took Corinna to the Savoy, a cousinly gesture which delighted that young lady. 'You have no idea how dull it is in the hospital,' she confided. 'Oh, I like the work, I really do, and when I've trained I shall come home and specialise in something or other.'

'No, you won't—you'll get married.'

'Well, yes, I intend to do that as well, but I'm not going to sit idle waiting for someone to come along and fall in love with me. You wouldn't if you were me, would you?'

'Certainly not. How much longer do you have to do?'

'Four months.'

He watched her spoon her raspberry sorbet and added, 'You can't leave before then?'

'Of course I can. Trained staff have contracts, or if they don't they have to give quite a long notice.'

'But students may not return and resume their training if they change their minds?'

'I'm not sure, but I shouldn't think so; if they did they'd have to lose training-time—make up whatever time they'd been away for. I didn't know you were interested in nurses?'

He shrugged. 'Idle curiosity.' He sat back while she studied the sweet trolley. Just for a moment he wondered if Caroline would enjoy dinner at the Savoy. No, not the Savoy, somewhere quiet and small…

'I shall have the trifle,' said Corinna. 'It's loaded with calories but it's mince tomorrow and I never eat that, so it won't matter.'

She gave him a wide smile across the table. 'You really are a dear, Marius. I got out quite a bit with some of the housemen, but they don't run to the Savoy.'

He took her back to the hospital and drove thoughtfully back to his house.

The next morning he went in search of Sister Crump. He found her with little Marc, checking his charts, and since he was asleep she went with him to her office.

'I shall be glad when Nurse Frisby gets back from nights off. I suppose it's a dull job, sitting with the child for hours on end, but they don't seem to have the good sense to stimulate him when he wakes. He's getting on well though. Have you come to see Mr Spence? He'll be here directly—it's his round.'

'Yes, I have, Sister, but I wanted to talk to you too.'

She sat down behind her desk and he took the only other chair in her office, a small wooden one which creaked alarmingly under his giant person.

'This may not be possible,' he began, 'but regarding little Marc's future treatment...' He talked for some time and Sister Crump listened without interrupting.

Only when she saw that he had finished speaking did she say, 'Well, it would be an ideal arrangement. Marc has always responded to her, you know, and she is—how shall I put it?—steadfast. It is possible for a nurse not to give up meticulous treatment upon an apparently moribund patient while in her mind she has convinced herself that it is useless. Nurse Frisby is like a bulldog; once she gets her teeth into something, she doesn't let go. We have her to thank for his recovery, I consider. Just sitting there day after day, enticing him back, if you see what I mean.'

For Sister Crump, who never spoke more than half
a dozen words at a time, this was an unusual speech.

'You will do all you can to further my idea?'

'Yes, most certainly. I pride myself on getting my
patients well, by whatever means. It remains for Mr
Spence to agree…'

'Oh, he'll agree. What about the nursing hierar-
chy?'

Sister Crump chuckled. 'There will be three of us…
but of course, Nurse Frisby has to agree without any
coercion.'

'Of course. I shall leave that to you and Mr
Spence.'

She shot him a thoughtful glance. 'Very well.' She
looked at the clock. 'He should be here at any moment.'

Mr Spence came into the office as she spoke.

He wished her good morning and turned to Mr van
Houben. 'Marius—the very man I wanted to talk to.
You will be going back to Holland in a day or two?
I think we should come to some decision about Marc,
don't you? I'm taking him off everything in easy
stages; we shall have to keep an eye on that lung for
a while but I'd like to get him back to normal life in
moderation. You agree? That means his return to his
own home, and to be on the safe side I'd like a nurse
with him for a period of time, depending on how he
gets on. Could you find a suitable nurse and drill her
before we send him back?'

'We were talking about that when you came in. What's wrong with sending Nurse Frisby home with him for a while? He responds to her more so than to any other person, other than his parents, of course. It might cause a bit of a set-back if we change his nurses midstream?'

Mr Spence nodded. 'I like the idea. What about Nurse Frisby?'

'She doesn't know anything about it,' Mr van Houben said blandly. 'She might possibly refuse— she would have every reason to do so; she is still training and I'm not sure how a period away from the hospital would affect that.'

'A special case?' Mr Spence looked at Sister Crump. 'What do you think, Sister?'

'I should have thought the two of you could bend the rules a bit. You'll need to get the SNO on your side. I think it's a good idea and I'm sure that if Nurse Frisby is approached in the right way she will agree. Whoever sees her had better be ready with all the answers—she's a quiet little thing, but no fool.' She glanced at the clock. 'No time like the present,' she said briskly. 'The SNO will be in her office for the next half-hour.'

Mr van Houben leaned over the desk and kissed her cheek. 'You're a jewel of a woman,' he told her. 'When I marry we shall have you for godmother for our eldest.'

'That's as likely as a pig flying,' she said, but all

the same she smiled widely. 'And remember to let me know what is to happen.'

Mr Spence was at the door. 'I'll be back,' he promised her.

Caroline had four nights off and the weather was kind, so that she could spend her days in the garden, planting seeds and bedding out the various things her aunt had nurtured in her tiny greenhouse; and when she wasn't doing that they shopped in a leisurely fashion in the village stores, and she and Aunt Meg went into Basingstoke and had a good prowl round Marks and Spencer, planning her spring wardrobe. Each morning, as soon as they had had breakfast and she had helped with the chores around the house, she took herself off on her bike and wandered round the ruins of Basing House. There wasn't much left of it, it had been looted and destroyed by fire during the Civil War, but there was a beautiful dovecote, quite undamaged, and the surrounding grounds were a pleasant place in which to wander. They had been excavated and yielded a rich harvest of Iron Age pottery, Roman coins and bits and pieces left over from the Civil War, and Caroline was always hopeful of finding something herself. Not that she looked very hard, but mooned around, enjoying the quiet and the splendid views, her thoughts vague and dreamy until she looked at her watch and remembered that she had promised to do the shopping and plant the wallflowers... Her aunt never reproached her if she had been away too long, only Theobald, sitting as usual in the porch, cast a reproachful eye upon her.

Three days didn't last forever, and the cumbersome pile of the hospital looked unwelcoming as she crossed the forecourt, thankful that she was on the morning shift for a week…

She went on duty at half-past seven the following morning, delighted to find that Marc had shed most of the paraphernalia to which he had been attached for so long. She took the report from the night nurse and was delighted when he woke up and smiled at her.

'Well, well, and what have you been doing since I saw you last?' she wanted to know.

He told her in his own language, of course, and she nodded and smiled and said, 'Well, well I never…' and tickled him gently so that he gurgled with delight.

Mr van Houben appraised of her arrival and approaching quietly, congratulated himself on the brilliance of his scheme. It merely remained for him to convince the girl that she would be rendering a vital service by going to Holland with Marc.

His good morning was casual but pleasant. Caroline, who hadn't expected to see him, murmured something as she sat down and he sat on the edge of the bed.

'I think we might have a talk,' he said, and smiled charmingly.

CHAPTER FOUR

'WHAT about?' asked Caroline, refusing to be charmed.

'Mr Spence considers that Marc is almost well enough to go back to his home in Holland—another week or ten days; he has suggested to me,' said Mr van Houben, lying with a calm face, 'that a suitable nurse should go with him—a new face might bother the little chap. It seems to be a good idea, do you not agree?'

'Well, yes, but it's nothing to do with me...'

'No, no, of course not. I expect you will be glad to get back to your usual ward duties.' He stayed a little longer but didn't mention the matter again and presently he went away, well satisfied. Unless he was mistaken, Caroline Frisby, seeds of the idea planted in her head, would be all the more willing to listen to Mr Spence, if only to take him down a peg for assuming that the thought of sending her with Marc had never entered his head. He strolled into Sister Crump's office and over coffee told her that he would be in touch with Mr Spence. 'I have to go back to Holland this evening,' he added, 'but I'll get him to talk to my sister—if Nurse Frisby agrees...' He smiled slowly. 'But she will, of course.'

Caroline, reciting 'Hickory, Dickory Dock' over and over again, because Marc found the bit about the mouse running up the clock irresistibly funny, allowed her thoughts to dwell on Mr van Houben. He hadn't said so, but it seemed to her that he didn't consider her suitable to go back with Marc to his home; indeed, he had implied that she was longing to go back to the ward. Of course, it was for Mr Spence to decide, but the pair of them seemed on very good terms and from what she had seen of Mr van Houben he possessed great powers of persuasion coupled with an ability to keep things to himself if he wished. Perhaps it was Nurse Foster he had in mind. Caroline left the mouse and the clock for the moment and started on 'Goosey Goosey Gander' for a change. Madge Foster was all right, she supposed—very clever theoretically, and quite unable to make a patient comfortable in bed. However, she was also a pretty girl; not only that, she had heard with her own ears Madge telling Marc's mother that she loved foreign languages; seemed to have an ear for them and had no difficulty in picking up the basics... 'The sly creature,' declared Caroline loudly, with the result that Marc laughed and brought her to her senses.

There was absolutely no point in getting annoyed; she wasn't even trained yet and Madge would be taking her finals in a few months.

Three days went by, and there was of course no sign of Mr van Houben. It wasn't until Marc's mother mentioned casually that he was in Holland that Caroline knew that. A good thing too, she reflected, always poking his nose in… That she missed him was something she had no intention of admitting even to herself.

Mr Spence came twice a day, but beyond routine questions and a polite hello and goodbye he had nothing to say to her, and Madge was looking very smug.

'Never mind how I know,' she whispered to Caroline before she went off duty, 'but a nurse is to go back with Marc to Holland—' she smiled in a pleased manner '—and I think it's going to be me. After all, I'm almost trained and I speak fluent French and German…'

'I thought they spoke Dutch in Holland,' said Caroline matter-of-factly, and Madge gave her a sharp look to see if she was being got at.

'Well, of course they do, but I'm very quick at languages; besides I've been top of my set for all the tests.' She paused to think. 'I wonder what kind of social life there is there?' She closed her lovely blue eyes for a moment and sighed happily. 'They're loaded, you know.'

Caroline chose to be dim. 'Who? The Dutch?'

'Don't be so stupid—Marc's people, of course.'

'Did you ask them?'

Madge turned to go. 'You're hopeless; no wonder none of the men will even look at you—your brain's as dull as your face.'

Caroline watched her go; if you were pretty enough you could get away with any amount of rudeness. All the same, remarks like that had a nasty habit at least of hovering at the back of one's mind.

She turned her attention to Marc and was sitting on his bed giving him his morning milk when Sister Crump and Mr Spence came in together.

It was after an unusually lengthy examination of the little boy that Mr Spence asked, 'Could a nurse be found to relieve Nurse Frisby for a little while? I should like to have a talk. You too, Sister.'

Caroline, following them out into the ward and into Sister Crump's office, wondered what she had done, and was still going over her various duties as Mr Spence politely stood aside to let her enter Sister Crump's office on the heels of that lady.

Inside she was offered the chair while he leant against the wall, his hands in his pockets. He stared at her in a rather intimidating way so she looked at Sister Crump, her hands quiet in her lap while her insides churned.

'Marc will be going home in a week's time,' said Mr Spence. 'I should like you to accompany him and stay for a couple of weeks while he adjusts to home life again. He likes you and his parents approve of you. They live in Alpen-aan-de-Rijn, which is near Leiden and is surrounded by very pretty country. Mevrouw van Houben would of course wish to talk to you should you agree to go with them to settle all the details and so on…'

'I wouldn't be allowed to go,' sighed Caroline. 'I'm not trained, sir, I'm only in my second year, and I'm not sure if I would be able to break my training.'

'That is a matter which I think can be dealt with satisfactorily if you agree to go with Marc. You would perhaps like a little time in which to think it over?'

Caroline knitted her mousy brows. 'No, I don't think so, thank you, sir. If you think it is a good idea for me to go back with Marc, then I'll go. As long as it doesn't interfere with my training.'

'Spoken like a sensible woman. I will see that you are kept informed, Nurse.'

At a nod from Sister Crump she went back to Marc, nettled at being called a sensible woman, although she was fair enough to assume that he had meant it as a compliment. Her feelings were soothed by Marc's pleasure at seeing her again. He was a dear little boy, still given to lapses of silence alternating with restlessness, but there was every chance that within a few weeks now he would be leading the normal life of a small boy of his age.

She telephoned to Aunt Meg when she got off duty and that lady expressed her satisfaction. 'Never mind if you have to make up the weeks you're away,' she said cheerfully. 'Obviously they think you're right for the job, so take it, love, it's an opportunity to see more of foreign parts. I envy you.'

The following day Mevrouw van Houben arrived just as Caroline had finished getting Marc ready for his day. She sat down in the comfortable chair by the bed and Caroline lifted Marc on to her lap with the advice that presently he could be taken for a brief walk around the ward.

'He gets a little giddy, but Mr Spence is quite satisfied. He can't go by himself, of course. Shall I get you a cup of coffee, *Mevrouw*?'

'No—no, thank you. Mr Spence has spoken to me of you, yes? So I have come to talk…'

Caroline was to have the care of Marc and no other duties, and after a week or so she was gradually to integrate him back into family life, always allowing for their doctor's approval. 'You will have him all day—you will not mind that? But each afternoon when he rests—does he not?—you will be free for an hour or so, and in the evenings if you wish to go out when he is in bed, someone will stay nearby him.' Emmie van Houben looked anxious. 'You will not mind this? Here in the hospital you have free days, but when you are with us I think that is not possible for a week or two and you will always be—how do you say?—on call.'

Caroline said in a reasonable voice, 'Well, I shan't know anyone in Holland, shall I? I mean, I won't want to go out socially. I think I shall be quite content with your arrangements, *Mevrouw*.'

All the same, despite her quiet reply, under her neat uniform her heart was pounding with excitement. Life until now had been uneventful, although happy. For some years she had had no illusions about her future; she had friends, but the young men she met had felt no urge to fall in love with her, and she could quite understand why. She had no clever conversation, she hadn't enough money to dress in the latest fashion and, over and above these drawbacks, she had no looks to speak of. Each by itself would have been overcome, but the three together…

Mevrouw van Houben heaved a sigh of relief. 'That's splendid. Mr Spence tells me that we may go home in five days' time. My husband will drive Nanny and the baby back, but we shall fly. An ambulance will take us to Heathrow and he has chartered a plane for us. We shall fly to Valkenburg airfield and be met by an ambulance and driven home. It is not far.'

Sister Crump gave her four days off; it was inconvenient, but she was fair enough to realise that Caroline would need to pack her things and go to her home. Caroline was very glad to go, since Madge, on hearing the news, had taken it as a personal insult and probably Caroline's fault that she had been passed over for the job. 'Heaven knows why they chose you,' she said bitingly. 'You won't understand a word anyone is saying and I dare say the upper classes speak French among themselves and, as you know, I'm rather good at languages.'

Caroline didn't say a word; she very much doubted that the Dutch would speak any other language than their own unless they needed to. The fact that she spoke passable French herself and even had a smattering of German wasn't worth mentioning. She made soothing replies and went to Basing to collect what she would need in the way of clothing.

She wasn't to wear uniform, Mevrouw van Houben had been adamant about that. Under Aunt Meg's kindly eye, she packed her blue denim skirt and several cotton blouses, a silvery grey cotton shirtwaister she had had for years, still elegant even if not in the forefront of fashion. Just in case the spring weather turned really warm, she added a flowered skirt and a cotton dress. A handful of woollies, the inevitable cardigan, a plastic mac and a second pair of shoes and she considered that then she was well equipped.

'Enough undies?' asked Aunt Meg. 'You never know…and what about something a bit dressy for the evening?'

'I won't need that—I'm sure I shan't have my meals with them.'

'How do you know that? A fine thing it would be if you turned up at the dinner table in a blouse and skirt and everyone else in silk crêpe and diamond earrings!'

'I don't think—' began Caroline.

'Well, good. We'll go into Basingstoke tomorrow morning and buy a dress.'

Aunt Meg was what one would call a sensible dresser, and Caroline, however much she drooled over the mini-skirts and vivid tops much in fashion, was aware that they hardly suited the occasion. After a good deal of to-ing and fro-ing, she settled on a pale green voile two-piece with a darker green pattern of leaves. A sensible buy, for she could wear the top as a blouse if she wished, and the skirt with one of her white blouses. It was as they did a final prowl round Marks and Spencer that she saw the cream silky top, loose and short-sleeved—just right with the skirt in the unlikely event of needing a change of outfits.

Very satisfied with her purchases, the two of them went back home, had their tea, fed Theobald and, since Caroline was going back to the hospital that evening, sat down to check that she had everything she would need. She prudently arranged to change some money into *gulden*, and it only remained to decide what to wear for the journey. Finally she unpacked the jersey dress; it wouldn't crush, and if it got messed up during travelling she could wash it, and since they were going by ambulance she wouldn't need to take a jacket or mac with her. She packed her shoulder-bag with everything she might need for the next twenty-four hours, locked her case and got into the local taxi, waved away by several of the neighbours as well as Aunt Meg and Theobald.

Caroline was on the ward, getting Marc ready for the journey soon after seven o'clock the next day. They weren't to leave until nine o'clock, but he became excited and unhappy if there was too much commotion around him. She gave him his breakfast, and, when Mevrouw van Houben arrived presently, went away to have her own meal in the company of various of her friends who had contrived to leave their wards on some errand or other.

'You'll have a heavenly time,' said Janey enviously. 'You'll meet a dashing Dutchman and come back engaged.'

There was a good-humoured laugh at that, and Caroline joined in, not in the least put out.

They left promptly, made an uneventful journey across London and out to the airport and were tenderly put aboard the plane. To Caroline, used to queues for tickets, Customs and baggage, it was a matter of surprise that travel should be so carefree. It was a relief, too, for Marc needed a good deal of attention; away from familiar surroundings he was inclined to be fretful, and it was only as they circled to land that he dropped off into a light doze. He stayed sleeping as they drove in the ambulance away from the airport, through Leiden and along the road running beside the Oude Rijn, then going through the town, to turn off on to a country road running between water meadows with here and there prosperous-looking farms lying well back from the road. They passed through two villages before Mevrouw van Houben said, 'We are nearly home. You see the lake? The village is close by.'

The village, when they reached it, was very small, a group of small houses, one or two fair-sized villas, a very large church and a tiny shop. The ambulance turned off into a narrow lane leading from the village square and turned into an open gateway between high walls and stopped before a square solid house set in a garden ablaze with spring flowers. Its door was flung open as the ambulance came to a halt and Mijnheer van Houben, followed by a stout elderly woman, came hurrying out. He embraced his wife and peered anxiously at his small son, still asleep, his head on Caroline's lap.

'He is well? Not sick? Is there any need for a doctor?'

'He seems perfectly well. I think if we could get him straight up to his bed—I'll get him undressed the moment he wakes…'

'Yes, that is best. I will carry him to his nursery and you will stay with him.'

Caroline following hard on the heels of the master of the house, had no time to look around; she had a fleeting impression of sombre panelled walls, a massive side-table with a clock, and two hideous matching vases, probably very valuable, upon it before she nipped smartly up the wide staircase leading to the gallery above, along a short passage and into a large sunny room at the back of the house. Bartus van Houben laid his son gently on to the bed.

'You will stay just for a short time? My wife will wish to see the baby, but then she will come and our housekeeper will show you your room and you will have time to unpack if you wish. There will be lunch shortly.'

It was half an hour before Mevrouw van Houben came, and in the meantime Marc had woken up, been undressed and put into his bed, where he lay holding Caroline's hand while she talked. He didn't understand, of course, but that didn't seem to matter; her soft voice was something with which he was familiar.

'He must eat,' said his mother. 'There is food ready for him, but you must eat also, Caroline. I have had lunch, so I will give him his meal while you have yours. Bep—the housekeeper—will take you to your room and show you where the dining-room is. It is a muddle for today; tomorrow we will be normal again.' Bep was the elderly woman who had come to the door with Bartus van Houben. She nodded and smiled at Caroline and led her across the passage to a pleasant room overlooking the side of the house, nicely furnished with a small bathroom leading from it. Caroline's case had been brought up and stood ready to be unpacked but that, she decided, could

wait. Breakfast had been a long time ago; she hoped
that lunch would be a satisfying meal…

It came up to expectations; an omelette, a basket
of bread and rolls, butter, cheese and a dish of ham
and cold meat, and a pot of coffee. She fell to and
was buttering a final roll when the door opened and
Marius van Houben sauntered in.

Caroline, her mouth full, uttered a surprised hello
in a thickened voice and wished that she didn't blush
so easily. At the same time she had to admit that she
was pleased to see him.

Mr van Houben swept a casual glance over her.
'No problems with Marc?' he wanted to know, and
waited with polite impatience while she swallowed
her mouthful.

Rude man, she reflected, he can't even say good
day. Out loud she said in a businesslike voice, 'None,
thank you, sir,' and poured herself another cup of coffee.

'Don't let me hurry you,' observed Mr van Houben
very evenly. 'When you have finished your meal I
should like to take a look at him.'

Caroline took a sip of coffee. She was, upon reflection, not in the least pleased to see him. Hopefully
he would go away presently and leave the family doctor, whoever he was, to take over the care of Marc.

She took another sip and he sat himself down on
the edge of the handsome table at which she was sitting. Rightfully she should have swallowed her coffee

and leapt to her feet, but she had no intention of being treated like a doormat. Too bad if he was a busy man…

She finished her coffee without haste and pushed back her chair.

'I'm ready when you are, sir,' she said politely.

He held the door open for her. As she went past him he said softly, 'Do not cross swords with me, young lady—you might come to grief.'

She judged it prudent not to answer that.

Marc had eaten his dinner and was lying quietly listening to his mother reading from a story-book, but she stopped as they went in, smiling at the sight of Mr van Houben, getting up to kiss him and talk at some length. Caroline, standing by, not understanding a word, waited quietly until he said, 'Well, shall we take a look, Nurse?'

Marc had no objections to being examined by his uncle, and Caroline had to admire the way he made a game of it, allowing the child to play with his stethoscope, teasing him gently so that he chuckled. He glanced at her. 'Everything seems in good shape.' He glanced at her. 'Continue the treatment he has been having, Nurse, but try letting him walk around for longer periods. An hour or so in the garden might be a good idea, but don't let him get tired.'

He turned away to speak to his sister-in-law and presently he went away, giving her a brief nod as he went, and when Mevrouw van Houben came back

Caroline asked, 'Is Mr van Houben to look after Marc, or do you have a family doctor?'

'Dr Berrevoet—he will come, he lives in the village, but Marius has always looked after Marc—he was born prematurely and for weeks he was never well—his chest was weak, but Marius made him better; he is so very good with children and has—how do you say it?—a technique with anaesthetics especially for children and for those who need special treatment with an anaesthetic. He is a very clever man.'

Caroline had already been told that several times; she wondered what he was like as a person. She would try and discover that while she was in Holland. Just out of curiosity, she hastened to remind herself.

Marc was restless and peevish for a few days; he still wasn't quite himself and Caroline had to acknowledge the good sense in sending her home with him; she was someone he knew, even if his surroundings were different. His mother and father spent as much time as possible with him, but the baby took up a good deal of Mevrouw van Houben's time and his father went early and frequently came back late, after Marc was asleep. All the same, he was making progress, talking more, happy to sit in the garden with Caroline carrying on the peculiar conversations which they held, each in their own language, playing simple childish games and walking to and fro on the lawn at the back of the house.

Caroline established some sort of routine within the first few days; it was obvious that Marc would need plenty of rest and she was firm about that, tucking him up in his bed after his midday dinner and then joining Mevrouw van Houben for lunch. She didn't dare leave the house or the gardens, not until he had settled down; she took a book into the garden and sat under the nursery window, ready to fly upstairs if he should need her. Actually, she didn't mind her lack of freedom. She wrote long letters to Aunt Meg and read several books about the local countryside which Mijnheer van Houben lent her, and in between whiles she just sat, daydreaming. Vague dreams, in which she lived in a lovely house in the country, wore beautiful clothes and was surrounded by handsome children, cats, dogs and the odd donkey and pony. There would be a car for her use, naturally, and she would speak fluent Dutch. There was a husband, of course; a dim figure in the background with nebulous features and an unlimited income. He tended to be very large, blue-eyed and handsome...

She would be roused from these fantasies by the family dog, Bruno, or the gardener, clipping the already neat hedges, or by Bep, with whom she had struck up a rather guarded acquaintance, and laugh at herself and admit silently that, although she was happy with the Van Houbens, the sooner she got back to her hard working life the better.

She saw Mr van Houben rather more often than

was good for her peace of mind, for despite her stern resolution not to let him intrude into her life she found it hard to do that. She did her best, though, greeting him with cool civility, giving him succinct reports as to Marc's progress; she even managed not to blush...

He came frequently, arriving unexpectedly and at any time of the day which suited him. On his third visit—at eight o'clock in the morning, while Caroline was bathing Marc—he sat on the damp edge of the bath while she dried the little boy, listening while she gave him details of Marc's progress during the last couple of days.

'Good.' He sauntered to the door. 'It is likely that you think that I am either distrustful of you or uncertain as to your ability to look after Marc. Neither— these visits have to be very carefully fitted in around my day's work.'

He nodded casually and went away, leaving the door open.

'I have never met such a man,' declared Caroline crossly to Marc, who giggled and then shouted with glee as his uncle put his head round the door.

'I choose to take that as a flattering remark, Caroline,' he told her silkily, and this time he shut the door after him.

She had been there just over a week when Mr Spence came. Mr van Houben arrived shortly after and the two men spent some time examining Marc while Caroline did as she was told, as professional as if she were in hospital, but presently she was left to dress him again while they went away to talk to his parents.

It was a pleasantly warm day; she carried Marc downstairs and into the garden, aware of voices coming from the drawing-room as she crossed the hall. Perhaps, she thought, they were deciding to tell her that she was no longer needed. Marc was making splendid progress now, and now that the new nanny had settled in Mevrouw van Houben had much more leisure to be with her small son.

She set Marc on his feet and walked him slowly across the lawn to the little summer-house at the end of the garden; it was a pretty, rustic affair which could be turned to face the sun or away from the wind. She swivelled it round so that they would be facing away from the house and sat down with Marc beside her and then, with an arm around his small person, opened the picture-book she had brought with her. It seemed to be a favourite of his and they recited the names of the various animals drawn on its pages, Marc's small voice sometimes a little slurred, and Caroline making heavy weather with the Dutch words.

'*Paard*,' recited Marc.

'Horse,' said Caroline, which made the little boy laugh.

'Never tell me that you jib at a few Dutch words,'

remarked Mr van Houben, appearing silently and sitting down beside Marc.

She cast him a cold look. 'Certainly not, but since there is no need for me to learn your extremely difficult language I see no reason why I shouldn't speak my own tongue when no one is listening.'

'Marc is listening and so am I.' He smiled suddenly, 'It is a difficult language to learn, you're quite right. I've come to fetch you back to the house. Mr Spence wants to talk to you.'

He stood up and hoisted his nephew on to a shoulder, and she perforce got up too and walked beside him across the lawn and in through the french windows of the drawing-room, where the van Houbens and Mr Spence were sitting drinking coffee.

'Come and sit,' invited Mevrouw van Houben, and beckoned her to go to the sofa beside her, 'and you will have a cup of coffee with us while we talk.'

So Caroline sat, aware that she showed up badly beside her companion, whose golden hair framed a charmingly made-up face and whose blue two-piece, unless Caroline was much mistaken, was cashmere. If I had known, she thought peevishly, I would have put on the jersey dress…

She accepted the coffee and glanced briefly at Mr van Houben, sitting opposite her with Marc on his knee.

It was Mr Spence who spoke. 'I am delighted with the progress Marc has made; he has still a long way to go but time is on his side, his lung seems to be healed and he eats and sleeps well. We think, Mr van Houben and I, that he should go into the children's hospital in Amsterdam for a brief period while we run a few tests. In order to see that he is disturbed as little as possible, we would like you to go with him. He knows you well now and you will be able to carry out all the usual chores which in the hands of a strange nurse might upset him. Mr van Houben can arrange for a bed in two days' time and his parents will drive you both to Amsterdam. You can appreciate that it is impossible for Mevrouw van Houben to stay with him; there is his little sister to consider.'

Mrs van Houben turned to Caroline and took her hand. 'You will do this, won't you, Caroline? I would like to be with Marc, but you can see that it is difficult while the baby is so very small.'

'Of course I'll go.' Caroline gave the hand a reassuring squeeze. 'And I'm so glad that he's making such good progress. You must all be so pleased and relieved…'

Mr van Houben offered Marc a biscuit. 'There is an EMI scanner at the hospital which means that most of the diagnostic techniques are unnecessary. He should be there a few days only. I suggest that nothing is said to him until a few hours before you leave.'

He looked at her as he spoke but it sounded as though he was doing a ward round and giving polite instructions to Sister. A cold fish, reflected Caroline, at the same time aware that he wasn't anything of the sort.

She went back to the garden presently with Marc, and at lunch, although both Mr Spence and Mr van Houben were careful to include her in the conversation, she sensed that they would have been just as happy without her. A pity, she thought, spooning soup, that she hadn't thought to suggest that she should have stayed with Marc after she had given him his dinner, and had something on a tray. Mevrouw van Houben was so kind that she would never have suggested it herself. She excused herself when the meal was over, refusing coffee on the grounds of making sure that Marc was asleep. 'Because if he isn't I will read to him for a while,' she explained.

Mr van Houben went to open the door for her; his manners, she had to admit, were faultless. 'Dutch or English?' he asked as she went past him.

'When there is no one to listen, Dutch. Marc is a very tolerant listener.'

His crack of laughter sounded annoyingly in her ears as she went upstairs.

Leaving the baby with her nanny, they were driven to Amsterdam two days later. It was a fine spring day, the country looked charming, and the gardens before the houses they passed were bright with flowers. Caroline, sitting at the back of the car with a cheerful Marc on her lap, wondered if she would have the chance to do some shopping; she had been paid be-

fore she left the hospital and so far she had spent
nothing save for a *gulden* or two on stamps. She was
wearing the jersey dress with a bright scarf knotted
at the neck, and in her bag she had packed the green
voile as well as the Marks and Spencer top to go with
the denim skirt. She had prudently added the plastic
mac, although she knew that it did nothing for her,
but she had the good sense to know that it rained very
frequently and the weather, if she was lucky enough
to get some time to go sightseeing, wasn't going to
keep her indoors.

They drove through a part of the city she had never
seen before, but after a little while she recognised
some of the buildings as those she had seen with Aunt
Meg and then got lost again as Bartus van Houben
drove away from the heart of the city towards the
Rhine, saying over his shoulder, 'The hospital is close
by. There is a frequent tram service to the shopping
centre.'

The hospital was right on the main road, its white
walls with its many windows rising rather bleakly
from the pavement, but once through the doors and
the gates at its side it looked more welcoming, with
a wide forecourt and a good-sized entrance. Bartus
stopped in front of it and got out with his wife, and
Caroline got out with Marc, carrying him, because he
had taken fright and buried his face against her shoulder.

She kept up a flow of gentle talk as they all went

inside and were taken upstairs at once in one of the lifts. Clearly they were expected, for no time was lost in asking where to go or whom to see: they were ushered into a small room on the second floor and a moment later a ward sister joined them. It was only then that Caroline wondered how she was going to manage about the language. Her Dutch, after so short a time, was about as basic as it could be, and presumably she would have to be told what was going on from time to time… A needless worry; Zuster Tregma introduced herself to the van Houbens and then she turned to Caroline.

'Miss Frisby, I am pleased to meet you. Do not worry about being understood. I speak English and the nurse who will relieve you while you are here also speaks good English.'

She looked at the back of Marc's head, still buried against Caroline. 'I think if we put him to bed, I will talk to Mijnheer and Mevrouw van Houben and presently Mr Spence and others will come. That will give him time to recover from his fears, will it not?'

So Caroline detached a reluctant Marc from her person and, with a good many pauses, singing and the odd five minutes here and there looking at one of his picture-books, she got him ready for bed. His mother came then and sat with him while Caroline saw where she was to sleep. A small room next door to Marc; someone had already put her bag there and she went to look out of the window. It overlooked the busy street below and she wondered where the nearest park was.

It only took a few minutes to unpack, tidy herself and go back to Marc. Mr Spence was there and so was Marius van Houben, sitting one each side of the bed, rumpling the covers and the little boy, quite recovered from his uneasiness, was laughing and shouting at their gentle teasing.

They got up as she went in. 'We'll have him up tomorrow afternoon, Nurse,' said Mr Spence. 'Arrange your off duty so that you will be with him, and I shall want to have you with him afterwards—he may be a little unsettled.'

Mr van Houben had nothing to say and presently they went away, but at the door he turned back. 'There is a small park close to the hospital,' he told her. 'Go left when you get to the main street and take the first turning on the left; it's five minutes' walk, no more. You will be glad of a breath of fresh air.'

Before she could thank him, he had gone.

CHAPTER FIVE

THERE was no chance of going to any park for the rest of that day: Marc's mother and father went away presently, leaving Caroline to look after Marc. He had become fretful at the sight of so many strange faces and clung to her like a limpet, so that she had spent the rest of the day with him, and not until he had finally fallen asleep in the early evening was she able to go down to the canteen with one of the Dutch nurses and eat her supper. When she went back to the ward the *hoofdzuster* came to talk to her. 'It will be difficult for you tomorrow,' she observed. 'Marc is restless without you or his mother. Do you wake early?'

Caroline said that yes, she did.

'Then it is a good idea, yes? If you are roused at six o'clock and go for half an hour to walk in the park—it is close by. Does Marc wake early?'

'About seven o'clock, but then he's usually asleep by half-past six. He's so unsettled now—' She glanced at her watch. 'It was well after seven o'clock before he slept this evening.'

'That is good. So you can walk before he wakes and if he is quieter tomorrow you will be able to have some free time during the day.' She nodded her severely coiffed head. 'A night nurse will be here within the next half-hour. Her English is good; tell her all that she should know. Someone will call you in the morning.' She went away to her office and Caroline went back to the sleeping Marc and presently, when she went off duty, she went to telephone to Mevrouw van Houben and assure her that her small son was asleep.

She went to bed early, for there was nothing else to do, so that she was quite ready to get up when she was called in the morning by a friendly night nurse bringing a mug of coffee. She was dressed and out of the hospital in fifteen minutes, intent on finding the park. It was a lovely morning, already light and getting warmer every minute under the sun beaming from the wide blue sky. She found the park without difficulty, less than five minutes' walk away from the hospital. It wasn't large, but there were trees and grass and beds of bright flowers on either side of its narrow paths, and here and there an inviting seat. There was a small fountain in the centre surrounded by a little pool. Sitting on its stone rim was Mr van Houben, and she stopped short at the sight of him, so very much at his ease. He, on the other hand, showed no surprise at seeing her, but got to his feet and came over to meet her.

'Good morning, Caroline.' He sounded friendly.

'Having a breath of air before the day's round? A delightful morning, isn't it?'

'Good morning,' said Caroline, pleased to see him but anxious now to show it. 'Yes, I am to go back in ten minutes or so, before Marc wakens. He's had a good night, the night nurse told me.'

'Come and sit down for a minute.' He pulled off the sweater he was wearing and arranged it on the rails. 'You'll come with him, of course. He is bound to get upset during the tests, but they must be done.'

'Do you think that he will make a complete recovery?'

'Yes, I do. It will be slow but that's to be expected, and it's possible that he may have the odd relapse— by that I mean a slight impairment of speech if he should get over-excited or very angry, and that isn't very likely. The main thing now is to get him used to being home again and back into his normal way of living. Emmie has a splendid woman engaged to be his governess for the next year or two; she will be introduced gradually of course, taking over from you in easy stages.' He glanced at her. 'You're quite happy here?'

'Yes, thank you.'

'A good thing, since you will be needed for another week or two at least. Juffrouw Grote is coming at the end of this week, provided the results of the EMI scanner are good.' He got to his feet and pulled her to hers, then picked up his sweater. 'Time you were going back.'

They walked together out of the little park and she paused there.

'I do hope all will go well, Mr van Houben.'

'It will, it will.' He didn't say goodbye but walked beside her back to the hospital. 'My car is parked round the back—I'll see you later.'

Marc was still asleep; Caroline had time for another cup of coffee and a slice of bread and butter thickly spread with cheese before he roused himself.

The tests went well; all the same Caroline was glad when it was at last the end of the day, for she hadn't been able to leave the little boy for more than brief periods. He was to spend one more day in hospital while final checks were made. Fortunately it *was* only one day, she thought as she tucked him up for the night, for he was fretful and wanting his mother and his own home. She bent to kiss him goodnight and he put his thin arms around her neck and gave her a throttling hug.

'Now be a darling boy and go to sleep and I'll sing "Sing a Song of Sixpence" to you and you shall sing it with me.'

He had picked up the words with the ease of a small child, although he had no idea what they meant, only the last line when a blackbird came along and pecked off her nose he sang with tremendous glee, sensing it was the high point of the rhyme. They sang

the last line with gusto and Mr van Houben, watching
from the doorway, smiled a little. Caroline, he reflected, was a funny little thing; no looks worth mentioning, a sharp tongue at times and, while not entirely careless of the way she looked, certainly not
fashion-conscious. She was, however, a good nurse;
his small nephew would make a complete recovery,
largely thanks to her care and wholehearted efforts.

He went into the room then, bade Marc goodnight
while casting a keen eye over him and then looked at
Caroline. 'Off duty?' he wanted to know. 'We might
have dinner together…'

He hadn't meant to say that, indeed he had no idea
what had made him utter the words, so it was all the
more puzzling that when she told him politely that
she was going out with some of the nurses he should
feel disappointment.

As for Caroline, she had uttered the lie with complete conviction. She would have liked above all
things to have spent the evening in his company, but
several good reasons had prompted her to refuse without hesitation; nothing to wear; the certainty in her
own mind that he had asked her on the spur of the
moment and was even now regretting it; a strange
reluctance to be in his company and the even stranger
wish to get to know him a lot better.

She watched him go away with mingled regret and
relief and presently, having handed Marc over, took
herself off to the canteen for supper. It was a lovely

evening, chilly but still light; she fetched her jacket and, after cautiously checking that there was no sign of Mr van Houben or his car, left the hospital.

The car was parked round the back, out of her sight, and Mr van Houben was standing at the window of the consultant's room, looking out, when he saw her. He watched her pause on the pavement outside the hospital and peruse the street map she had prudently taken with her before setting out towards the centre of the city. There was no sign of anyone with her; she looked small and lonely as she started to walk. She hadn't gone more than a few yards when two men stopped to speak to her; he watched her shake her head and then walk on briskly, leaving the two men laughing.

Mr van Houben sighed and went out of the room, out of the hospital and into the street beyond. Caroline was walking faster now, pausing at each crossing to make sure that she was going in the right direction. They would probably be gone tomorrow, she had decided, and this was her only chance of seeing something of Amsterdam again. Aunt Meg would want to know where she had been and it was a chance to see what the city was like after dark. She remembered that their guide-book had said that the Rembrandt-splein was ringed around with cafés—she would go there, have a cup of coffee and then walk back or even take a tram...

There were plenty of people about and the streets

were well lit, and she had no intention of leaving the main road. She walked on, pausing now and again to look at a picturesque house or a stretch of canal. Once or twice people spoke to her, but when she took no notice they melted away into the crowds. She wasn't a nervous girl, she had little money with her and there was nothing about her unassuming person to attract attention, but as the crowds grew thicker she wondered if she should have come so far alone. She stopped again to look at the map under a street lamp. Rembrandtsplein was close; it would be a great pity to have come this far and not seen it so that she could describe it to Aunt Meg. She walked on and found her way barred by a young man. He was ill-kempt, with a dirty face and long greasy hair, and naturally enough when he spoke to her she had no idea what he was saying.

She removed his grubby hand from her sleeve. 'So sorry, I don't speak Dutch,' she told him, and made to pass him. His hand took a firmer grip and she didn't care for his smile. 'Let go, please,' she said in what she hoped was a firm voice, which didn't help at all, for he gripped her other arm as well. She had no wish to make a scene and for all she knew she thought he might be asking her for money. Unfortunately she couldn't get at the purse in her jacket pocket. 'Take your hands away, please,' she told him in a voice which shook just a little, 'or I shall be forced to call for help.'

It seemed most unlikely that anyone would hear or take any notice; there were a good many young people darting about making a lot of noise, arms entwined or arm-in-arm singing; all the same it was worth a try. She opened her mouth and drew a breath just as Mr van Houben said gently in her ear, 'No need to scream, Caroline,' and addressed himself to the man, who muttered uncertainly and then disappeared into the crowd.

Relief flooded her person but so did indignation. 'I had no intention of screaming,' she said with a snap. 'I was merely going to call for help.'

He tucked a hand under her arm. 'You're a long way from the hospital—we might as well have a cup of coffee before we go back. Were you making for the Rembrandtsplein?' When she nodded, he went on easily, 'Quite a tourist attraction. Did you go there with your aunt at all?'

She quelled an absurd wish to burst into tears. 'Only during the day; I—I thought I would like to see it lit up, then I can tell her about it.'

'Good idea.' They had reached the square now, its cafés and restaurants spilling out on to the pavements and thronged with people. He passed these and ushered her into the foyer of the Canansa Crest Hotel, which, while bustling and brilliantly lit, was entirely respectable, something which Caroline noticed at once and for which she gave him a shy grateful smile.

'It's rather—that is, I didn't know that it was so popular—the Rembrandtsplein, I mean.'

He ordered coffee and sat back at his ease, and she waited uneasily for him to ask her what she thought she was doing roaming around a strange city in the evening. Probably he would read her a lecture into the bargain...

He didn't mention it, but while they drank their coffee he talked of this and that in an offhand fashion which was somehow reassuring. She wasn't going to admit it, even to herself, but she had had a bad fright when that man had caught her by the arm; she would thank Mr van Houben when they got back to the hospital, and apologise.

They walked back presently, this time through small quiet streets, and when they reached the hospital she bade him a quiet goodnight and added, 'Thank you for sending that man away; it was very silly of me to go off on my own...'

'Why? I suspect that you are perfectly capable of looking after yourself, Caroline. But it was very silly of you to lie to me—don't ever do it again. Goodnight.'

He pushed open the door for her and she went past him, her cheeks red and angry tears in her eyes. He was quite right, of course, but he need not have sounded so coldly angry.

They went back to Alpen-aan-de-Rijn the next day, fetched by Mijnheer van Houben and seen off by several of her new acquaintances among the nursing staff.

'You must come to Amsterdam again,' said Mijnheer van Houben kindly. 'You have made friends and you can perhaps spend a day sightseeing with them. You will have some free time now that Juffrouw Grote is engaged as governess. She will come each afternoon at first, when Marc wakes from his nap, and stay with him until teatime, and then after a few days she will come in the morning until his lunchtime, and then, if all is well, she will come all day. We hope that you will stay with us for the next ten days or so, Caroline, so that he will be quite used to her by then. He is fond of you, so it would not do for you to leave suddenly, Marius agrees with me about that, and so does Mr Spence. You do not mind?'

She said that of course she didn't mind; there was nothing else she could have said, after all; it was a sensible solution and little Marc was also almost ready for a normal life again.

Juffrouw Grote arrived the next day, a generously built girl with a pleasant, kind face, not much older than Caroline. Caroline liked her at once and, invited to help her unpack, sat on the bed, giving Juffrouw Grote a succinct résumé of Marc's accident and its consequences, and, since her successor's English was more than adequate, she was able to add a good many ideas and tips of her own.

'I can't go on calling you Juffrouw Grote,' said Caroline. 'My name is Caroline…'

'Tine—Te-ne. I shall ask the little Marc to address me as that also. I am told that he is very fond of you.'

'Only because I've been with him for some time. He's a very loveable little boy; I'm sure he'll take to you.'

'Take to me?! I do not understand.'

Caroline explained. 'I expect you will see Mr Spence before he goes back to England.'

Tine nodded. 'Yes, I am to see him tomorrow and also Mijnheer van Houben, but today I am to stay with Marc for the afternoon—you know this already.'

Caroline, who had been a bit doubtful about handing over to someone she didn't know, heaved a sigh of relief—she and Tine liked each other and she couldn't leave little Marc in better hands. Tine had lunch with them presently and Marc, wary at first, decided that he liked her too and went off happily enough with Caroline for his nap knowing that when he woke up it would be Tine who would see to his small wants. Caroline, said Tine cheerfully, was going to have a walk that afternoon, but she would be back in plenty of time to give him his tea.

The new regime worked well; each day Caroline saw a little less of Marc and Tine saw more, and by the end of a week she was getting him up each morning and giving him breakfast with Tine and herself and then handing him over until the afternoon with no ill effects. He had grizzled a bit to start with but he liked Tine and slowly he was becoming accustomed to seeing more of her than of Caroline.

Another week, reflected Caroline, walking down to the village to buy postcards and stamps, and she would leave; Mr Spence was coming that afternoon and she expected to be told that she was no longer needed. Indeed, she was beginning to feel that she was quite surplus in the household, although the van Houbens treated her with great kindness and made no mention of her leaving. But that afternoon Mr Spence put an end to her speculations. She might return to the hospital at the end of the next week; Juffrouw Grote was coping admirably with Marc, the van Houbens were quite satisfied that she was a kind and caring girl and observant of any unlikely set-backs he might have. 'No doubt they will arrange your return to London,' he told her, 'and I have had a talk with the hospital committee and they are inclined to be lenient about your absence. Possibly you may need to work for an extra month; they will deal with that when the time comes.'

Not very satisfactory from her point of view, but one didn't argue with consultants; she would go and see the SNO when she got back and find out exactly where she stood. She was bidding Mr Spence a polite if rather cold goodbye when Mr van Houben joined them.

'Still here?' he wanted to know cheerfully and, not

waiting for her reply, 'Everything as it should be?' he enquired of Mr Spence. 'I hear from Emmie that Juffrouw Grote is ideal for the job.' He glanced at Caroline. 'Get on well together, do you?'

'Yes, thank you.'

'Splendid. Well, we won't keep you—I dare say I shall see you from time to time at the hospital.'

She eyed him thoughtfully. 'I think it unlikely that you see—actually see—any of the junior nurses, sir. Good afternoon, Mr Spence—Mr van Houben.'

She made a dignified exit, her back very straight. The two men stared after her for a moment and then fell to discussing the patient's condition. Neither of them gave her another thought, only as Mr van Houben got into his car he reflected that she had been quite right, he rarely actually looked at any of the nurses—ward sisters occasionally, and staff nurses, since he had to discuss cases with them. He smiled a little; he must remember next time he was in London to make a point of singling her out and speaking to her.

He drove himself home to Amsterdam, changed for the evening and took a charming widow of his acquaintance out to dinner. She was an amusing companion and very pretty, but rather to his surprise he found himself wishing that it were Caroline sitting opposite him. He dismissed the thought with a hidden smile; small, energetic young women with a fund of common sense and a complete disregard for making the most of themselves were hardly to his taste.

He drove his companion home presently, refusing in the nicest possible way to go in and have a cup of coffee. He wasn't a conceited man but he was aware that women liked him, and not only him: his wealth, his background, his important work in the medical field…work which, however, filled his days and his powerful mind. It would have to be a girl in a million to make him change his mind and marry.

He let himself into his lovely old house by the canal and went along to his study, followed by Fram and a small untidy-looking dog. Mr van Houben glanced down at the beast and bent to pat him. 'He's no trouble, Fram?'

'None, *mijnheer*. A grateful animal too, and so he should be.'

Mr van Houben sat down at his desk and the little dog settled by him, looking up adoringly into his face. 'He'll soon have a name?'

'Something watery,' suggested Fram, 'Anna thought, seeing that you fished him out of a canal. Shall I bring you a nice cup of coffee, *mijnheer*?'

'Yes, please. We'll call him Neptune—he came out of the deep, didn't he?'

Fram allowed himself a dignified smile. 'Oh, very good, *mijnheer*.' He then went away to tell Anna and fetch a tray of coffee. He had been with the family a very long time and he had a strong affection for

Marius; he said now as Anna added wafer-thin biscuits to the tray. 'A pity he can't find a good wife, but he'll be hard to please.'

'He'll meet his match one day,' said Anna comfortably, and for no reason at all remembered the English girl who had fallen down outside the house. It would have surprised her very much to know that Mr van Houben was remembering her too, sitting in his chair, doing nothing. He had a heavy schedule ahead of him for the next week or two but at the moment he wasn't concerned with it, he was in fact making plans, with his usual meticulous attention to detail, to take Caroline out for the day before she returned to England.

He addressed the little dog. 'You see, Nep, she had very little fun while she's been here and it isn't possible for Emmie and Bartus to spend a day away from home.'

Nep thumped a straggly tail. 'You agree with me? She isn't quite whom I would choose to spend the day with, but one must do what one considers is one's duty.' He added, 'There is, of course, the possibility that she will refuse to come; I'm not sure that she likes me.'

Neptune licked the large elegant shoe he was leaning against as if to say that he for one could find no fault with the shoe's wearer.

Caroline had time to herself now as Tine took over more and more of her day's work, but beyond going into Alpen-aan-de-Rijn to look at the shops and buy a modest present for Aunt Meg she hadn't gone far away. For one thing she hadn't a great deal of money left. She was to fly back; Mr van Houben had given her her ticket, assured her that he would drive her to Schiphol himself, and written down the time of the flight so that she could make her own arrangements when she reached Heathrow, but there would still be some small expenses and she would have to get back to the hospital from the airport. She didn't allow it to worry her; it was nice to have a few hours each day in which to explore and Bep actually lent her an old bicycle and she tooled around the bicycle paths, safe from the traffic, admiring the very pleasant countryside.

There was still plenty for her to do; Marc, now that he was almost well again, was frequently peevish and when that happened she and Tine took it in turns to amuse him, take him for short walks or read to him, but he slept through the night now so that the two of them, after dining with the van Houbens, were able to sit together and talk.

Mr van Houben came twice, the first time with Mr Spence, before the surgeon returned to London, the second time alone. Both times Caroline was out on the bike. When Tine mentioned it she felt regret mixed with relief that she hadn't seen him again. They had, after all, said goodbye, and, as she had pointed out so sensibly to him, even if they saw each other in the hospital, there would be no reason for them to speak to each other.

However, he came a third time, two days before she was due to go home, and this time she was with Marc when he came into the nursery with his sister.

She was on the floor, teaching the little boy to play marbles, and the pair of them scrambled to their feet, he to run to his mother and uncle, she to stand composedly, her dress rumpled and her hair anyhow. Not that it mattered, she reflected, watching Mr van Houben with his nephew. Presumably he was either coming or going to hospital—or possibly he had a private practice as well—for he was wearing a sober grey suit and a silk tie which probably had cost more than the dress she was wearing. He looked very handsome, self-assured and a little remote; indeed his, 'Good morning, Caroline,' had been uttered in a polite impersonal tone.

Her own reply had been suitably colourless.

He came to stand by her presently, his nephew clinging to one long trouser-leg. 'You return home on the day after tomorrow?'

He knew that already—hadn't he bidden her good-bye only a few days ago?

'Yes.'

'If you are free tomorrow I should be delighted to show you more of Amsterdam and anywhere else you would like to see.'

He watched the utter astonishment on her face followed by a slightly mulish expression—she was going to refuse. Indeed she had her mouth open to frame a polite reply when Mevrouw van Houben exclaimed happily, 'Is that not a splendid idea, Caroline? There must be a good deal that you have not yet seen, and Marius is a splendid guide. Such a nice end to your stay with us. What time will you come, Marius?'

'Half-past nine? If that suits you, Caroline?' said Mr van Houben blandly.

She had thought up several good reasons for not going while at the same time at the back of her head was the nagging thought that she wanted to go very much. 'I've one or two presents still to buy,' she began—not true, of course, but she hoped she sounded convincing. 'And my packing to finish.'

'Marius will take you to the shops,' declared his sister-in-law, 'and I'm sure your packing won't take more than half an hour—you're not going until after lunch. You will so enjoy yourself, Caroline.'

Caroline doubted that, and, as for Mr van Houben, she very much doubted if he would find enjoyment in her company—and for how long? And what would they talk about?

Mr van Houben, in his most persuasive voice but with a note of steel in it, said casually, 'Well, that's settled. I'll be here and see you at half-past nine.'

They stayed a little longer, and when they had gone, taking Marc with them for a stroll in the garden, Caroline went in search of Tine, who was washing

her smalls in the bathroom they shared. She listened
to Caroline's news with smiling pleasure. 'So nice for
you, you will have a good day with Mr van Houben
and fine memories of Holland when you leave. I shall
be sorry that you go but we must write to each other.
You will be glad to finish your training and then you
will be free to do as you wish, yes? Come back to
Holland and visit—you know us all—we shall all
welcome you.'

Caroline wondered if Mr van Houben would welcome her—well, he'd do that because he had nice
manners, but she thought it would only be a frosty
welcome…

She said, 'What shall I wear? Tomorrow…'

'You will be in the car? Then wear the silk top and
that pretty green skirt and, since you are an English
lady, you will take a cardigan with you.'

'Well, yes, I suppose that would do—I've got that
cream wool one.' She sighed—he wouldn't notice
anyway.

She was mistaken, Mr van Houben standing in his
sister-in-law's hall, watched Caroline coming down
the staircase and found to his surprise that he ap-
proved of what he saw; probably Marks and Spencer,
he judged, but chosen with an eye to the general ef-
fect. Clever, too; the outfit would pass muster anywhere.

She had done her face with extra care but it didn't
need much; she had a lovely creamy skin and she had

borrowed one of Tine's lipsticks for her too wide, gentle mouth. The eyes needed nothing, framed in curling lashes—looking at them, he reflected, one forgot the unassuming face…

Farewells said, he stowed her into the car, got in beside her and drove back to Amsterdam. It was a glorious spring morning, although there was a cool breeze and the country was serene and flat and somehow soothing.

Her companion glanced at her, sitting very composed beside him. 'Is there anything you missed when you were here with your aunt?' he asked. 'I thought a stroll round Amsterdam, perhaps? You won't mind if we go to my house first? I must pick up Neptune.'

She turned to look at him. 'Oh—a dog?'

'Yes—well, a puppy still.'

'That's a strange name…'

'We call him Nep.'

Who is we? wondered Caroline, and made one of her sensible remarks about the weather.

The house was just as lovely as she had remembered it, and the old man who opened the door to them was just as dignified. They were barely inside before there was a scrabbling from behind the baize door at the end of the hall and Nep rushed to meet them.

Caroline sank to the floor and hugged the little beast. 'He's beautiful,' she cried, 'and he's laughing. Have you had him long?'

'A few weeks.' He stood watching her; she was quite unselfconscious, absorbed in the little dog. He turned to Fram and asked for coffee in a quiet voice. Fram went away to the kitchen to state in his dignified way that the English miss who had fallen down outside the house earlier that year was in the house, a guest of the good doctor. 'And a very nice young lady she is,' said Fram, 'though she is not pretty.'

'Come and have coffee,' invited Mr van Houben at his most urbane. 'Would you object to Nep in the car? I thought that after lunch we might drive around here and there.'

'Where?' asked Caroline, getting up and going into a large lofty room with Nep prancing between them.

'You haven't seen the Keukenhof, have you?' and when she nodded he went on, 'but not the Linnaeushof? Shrubs and trees as well as flowers in season? I prefer it to the Keukenhof although it isn't as colourful. And Haarlem—did you go there? No? Then we will go and look at the market square; there is some fine architecture there.'

As he talked, he ushered her to a chair by the open window at the back of the house overlooking a surprisingly large garden, long and narrow.

'Not all the houses have gardens,' he explained, sitting down opposite her while Nep arranged himself across his shoes. 'My ancestor was one of the lucky ones.'

She allowed her eyes to roam around the room; it

was very beautiful, with a vast stone hood over the
fireplace, panelled walls hung with a great many
paintings and two bow-fronted display cabinets filled
with china and silver. Very grand, she decided, and
gave a surprised look at the basket in a corner of the
room in which a cat lay curled around three sleeping
kittens. Somehow it made the room a friendly place
despite its magnificence.

'That's Jane—nothing to look at but a charming
character and a splendid mother. Ah, here is the coffee—will you pour?'

While they drank it he suggested a number of
places she might like to see. 'All within walking distance; we will come back here for lunch and then take
the car. Unless there is anything you would prefer?'

She shook her head and was presently borne away
by Fram's wife to tidy herself before setting out from
the house, leaving a doleful little dog in the hall. Mr
van Houben saw her backward glance. 'He will come
with us this afternoon,' he promised.

He took her first to the Willet Holthuysen Museum
on the Herengracht, only a short distance away—a
seventeenth-century merchant's house where she
could have lingered for hours but, urged on by fresh
delights in store, they walked the short distance to
Waterlooplein and spent half an hour at the flea market, where Caroline bought a small Delft plate. When
she admired a painted papier mâché box, he bought
that too. 'A small memento of Holland,' he told her

casually. He took her to the antiques shops next, strolling through narrow little streets lined with even narrower shops, their windows filled with a miscellany of treasures.

Caroline, her small nose quivering with a wish to see everything at once, went from shop to shop while he patiently translated prices and the names of the window's contents, amused at her absorption and to his surprise enjoying himself.

Lunch was waiting when they got back: cucumber soup, grilled sole stuffed with shrimps, and strawberries and cream. At her look of pleased surprised Mr van Houben murmured, 'I know someone with glass houses.'

He had learnt, years ago, how to put people at their ease, and he was succeeding very nicely with Caroline. She had lost her shyness and the rather stilted conversations she had offered became normal, so that he was able to draw her out and presently listen to her answering the questions he asked until she said abruptly, 'I'm talking too much about me, I'm sorry.'

He had smiled at her then, a kind smile which set her at ease again.

Linneaushof was delightful, its flower-beds laid out informally, the trees and shrubs newly green. It had turned quite warm and they wandered along its paths with Nep trotting on the end of his lead until Mr van

Houben suggested that since they were so near they might as well take a look at the sea.

He drove her to a very small village behind the dunes, left the car and, with Nep running free, walked her along the smooth sands, stretching north and south as far as her eyes could see. It was almost chilly in the wind coming off the sea but the air had given her a lovely colour and her severely pinned hair had become a little loose. She was happy, happier than she had been for a long time, and she wasn't sure why, but suddenly life was wonderful and exciting. They didn't talk much but the silence was a friendly one and she no longer felt that she had to say something, no matter what. She could have stayed there for hours but presently they retraced their steps and got back into the car.

'Tea?' asked Mr van Houben, and drove to Haarlem.

He took her to Le Chat Noir and gave her an elegant tea with a selection of cakes to satisfy the fussiest of appetites, and when they had finished he took her to Market Square to show her the lovely old houses lining it and then he drove her back to Alpen-aan-de-Rijn in time for dinner. There she thanked him for her lovely day. 'You have been very kind and I enjoyed it,' she told him in her quiet voice, while the unbidden thought that probably he was glad to be rid of her went through her head. As though she had voiced the thought out loud he said, 'I should have liked to take you out to dinner but I have several appointments this evening.'

'You have given me more than enough of your time.' Her grey eyes, with their incredible lashes, stared up into his face. 'I'm most grateful. Don't let me keep you—you mustn't be late.'

He thought of the two meetings he had to attend that evening before going to a reception at the Burgermeester's house and found himself wishing that he was spending it with her. He said casually, 'Will you tell Emmie that I'll phone her in the morning? Goodnight, Caroline.'

'Goodbye, Mr van Houben.'

It really was goodbye this time. He drove away without a backward glance and she went into the house. Everyone was in the drawing-room but just for a moment she wanted to be alone. She had discovered something, and she was trembling with the discovery. She had just said goodbye to the man she loved; she had only just discovered that too. It left her shaken and suddenly unhappy, all the lovely euphoria of the day swept away, for was there anything more hopeless than loving a man who didn't look at one except to smile kindly and rather vaguely? As though I were one of his patients, thought poor Caroline.

She took a deep breath and opened the drawing-room door. Life had to go on.

CHAPTER SIX

PARTING from little Marc wasn't easy, Caroline had grown fond of him over the weeks and he of her. Although they had been careful to tell him that she would be leaving him, when the actual moment of parting came he burst into tears and became so upset that nothing else would do but to promise him that she would come and see him again soon—a promise made by his father and which, on their way to Schiphol, he reiterated to Caroline. 'You would not mind?' he asked, 'if we were to send you your ticket to fly over and spend a few days with us? There was no chance to ask you, but you could see for yourself that Marc was upset and that was all that I could think of.'

'Of course I'll come, but please give me plenty of warning, for I would have to ask for leave—just for a few days...'

In those few days, she thought, she might see Mr van Houben or at least hear of him. The future, which had looked bleakly empty, held a tiny glimmer of light now.

Bartus van Houben went as far as he could at the airport, leaving her finally with an armful of magazines and an envelope tucked into her handbag. She opened it once they were airborne and found a cheque inside—a generous one—accompanied by a charming letter of thanks. She hadn't expected that; they had been more than kind to her while she had been with them and her duties had been light, even if the hours were sometimes long and irregular. She spent the short flight planning how she would spend the money, much hindered by thoughts of Mr van Houben.

The hospital, after the extremely comfortable surroundings in which she had been living, looked awful; Caroline wanted to turn and run as she got out of the taxi and looked up at its gloomy pile, but once she was inside and in the nurses' home, being greeted by such of her friends as were off duty, it didn't seem so bad after all. Then she reminded herself sensibly that she had been lucky enough to enjoy several weeks of gracious living and she must be thankful for that, never mind that her heart was breaking because she would never see Mr van Houben again—well, she would see him, of course, but it wouldn't be the same; he would forget her soon enough. Indeed, she wondered if she had made sufficient impression upon him for him to have anything to forget.

Mindful of Home Sister's injunction that she was to report to the office as soon as she got in, she made her way downstairs to the main block where the SNO had her office, flanked by her two deputies and a formidable secretary. It was after six o'clock by now and all the ladies looked as though they needed a rest from their various tasks but the Senior Nursing Officer received her kindly enough, observed that it was a feather in the hospital's cap that little Marc should have made a recovery, and said that, since Caroline had fulfilled the task she had been given by Mr Spence in a satisfactory manner, the hospital committee were pleased to allow her to take her final assessment provided she made up the time she had been away afterwards.

She offered this news with the air of one conferring a genuine favour, and Caroline supposed that it was and did her best to look suitably grateful. The SNO's next piece of news, that she was to return to the children's ward, under Sister Crump, did cheer her up, however, and so did the advice that she might take four days off at the end of the week.

She phoned Aunt Meg with the news before she went to bed and then, fortified by several cups of tea and a good gossip catching up with the hospital news, she slept, and just before she did so she thought of Mr van Houben and wondered what he was doing.

He was sitting at his desk correcting examination papers submitted by the first-year medical students at Leiden Medical School; he was wholly engrossed, frowning and tut-tutting and writing terse remarks in the margins, and he hadn't spared her a thought.

Sister Crump was pleased to see her in the morning. 'A nice little job of work, Nurse Frisby—only what I would have expected from one of my nurses, mind you, but all the same I'm pleased with you. We're busy and I want some of the cots moved and it's Mr Spence's round so don't dawdle.'

It fell to her lot to make beds with Madge Foster, who was still smarting at the injustice of being overlooked by Mr Spence. 'I dare say you wouldn't have any fun,' she said spitefully. 'I mean, if you haven't any idea what people are talking about, it must have been pretty dull.'

'Not a bit of it,' said Caroline cheerfully, 'everyone spoke English, even the butler…'

'Butler? Was there a butler? But you didn't actually *meet* people?'

'Any number—the nurses at the children's hospital in Amsterdam were very friendly and I had the chance to look around the city too.' She paused, not wishing to say any more about that and then went on, 'The van Houbens had a lovely house just outside a charming little town—they had lots of friends, too…'

'You didn't speak to them, though…'

'Well, of course I did; there were guests to dinner most evenings.' Which was a slight exaggeration, but Madge deserved that. 'And I had lunch and dinner with the family. Marc had a lovely nursery and before I left his new governess took over—we got on awfully well.'

'Did you see Mr Spence?'

'Oh, yes—he came over twice.'

'I suppose he talked to you too,' sneered Madge.

'Well, of course he did—about Marc.' She mitred her corner of the sheet carefully and, the last cot seen too, went to help with the mid-morning feeds.

She was sitting patiently with a six-week-old baby who had neither the inclination or the energy to feed, so that every drop needed to be coaxed into his small mouth, when Mr Spence paused by her chair.

'Back at work, I see, Nurse—er—Frisby. You had a good journey back?'

'Yes, thank you, sir.'

'Did you leave Marc in good spirits?'

'Oh, yes—a bit put out that I was leaving, but he loves Tine, his new governess.'

'Good, good, splendid.' Mr Spence looked as if he wanted to say more but wasn't sure what. He nodded at her and gave her a wintry smile and moved away to the next patient and Caroline continued tickling the baby under its tiny chin, encouraging it to swallow while she thought about Mr van Houben. How would she feel if he were to come through the ward door at that very moment? Delighted to see him, of course, but what would be the point? What, indeed, was the point of being in love with a man with whom one had nothing in common?

The baby opened its eyes and stared up at her and she kissed the top of its bald head; he wasn't a pretty baby and he had that pugnacious look and a nasty temper; he would probably turn into a tiresome little boy. 'And good luck to you, poppet,' said Caroline, urging down the last of his feed. 'You're putting up a good fight...'

She lifted him over her shoulder to burp and went on talking to him, since there was no one there to listen. 'And if you can put up a fight I don't see why I can't—I can but try.' Her lovely eyes narrowed. 'I could have something done to my hair and buy some make-up and some clothes—there's that cheque, even if I do give Aunt Meg some of it.'

The baby blew a very small raspberry into her ear and she laughed then and took him away to change him and put him back into his cot.

The prospect of four days off made the rest of the week go quickly enough. She packed her weekend bag, wrapped the plate she had bought in the flea market and caught an evening train from Waterloo, and, since she had been paid, she took a taxi to Basing in time for a late supper with Aunt Meg.

They sat at the kitchen table with Theobald between them, eating one of Aunt Meg's steak and kidney pies while Caroline gave a detailed account of her stay in Holland. When she had finished, having skimmed lightly over any mention of Mr van Houben, Aunt Meg observed, 'Well, isn't that most satisfactory, love? Getting the little boy well again and you having such a nice time too. You said you saw Mr Spence there, and Mr van Houben too I dare say—I expect he was anxious about the little lad.'

'He came from time to time, sometimes with Mr Spence.'

Her aunt gave her a thoughtful look. 'And how kind of the little boy's father to give you a present. You must go shopping, love—some dresses and shoes, and Marks and Spencer have some lovely undies.'

'You're going to have a new dress too,' said Caroline, 'There's plenty of money for both of us. We'll go tomorrow, shall we?' She paused. 'I thought I'd go to the hairdresser's too.'

'What a good idea—there's that new salon—you know the one I mean? You could ring up and make an appointment before we go in the morning.'

They got home the next evening with not a penny left of the cheque. Aunt Meg had her dress and for once had consented to choose a colour other than her usual useful beige. Blue, a soft blue, and the material was soft too, and made up in a style suited to her sturdy frame. As for Caroline, she had remembered her resolution and cast good sense to the winds. She had made a beeline for Laura Ashley and returned to Basing laden with a most satisfying collection of garments: a pale pink dress with a wide lace collar, a navy and white dress with a little navy jacket to go on top of it, an assortment of well-cut T-shirts, a flowered skirt in raspberry-pink and a white cotton blouse of fine lawn, lavishly embroidered, and there had been money enough to buy a pair of low-heeled sandals.

She had been to the hairdresser too and had her hair cut and washed and dressed most becomingly in a french pleat. Trying everything on that evening, she wished that Mr van Houben could see her now.

She hadn't intended to take any of her new finery back to the hospital, but it was Aunt Meg who persuaded her. 'Take the lot,' she advised in her sensible way. 'Why leave them hanging in the cupboard here? Wear them just for the pleasure of it, love, and you can leave those dresses from I don't know how many years back and I'll take them along to Oxfam or one of the charity shops. If you haven't got them you can't wear them,' she added triumphantly.

So Caroline took her new wardrobe back to London and hung it in her bedroom cupboard and wondered when she would wear it; the T-shirts and the flowered skirt would do very nicely for off duty, but the pink dress was something special, so was the navy and white outfit, and special occasions only rarely came her way.

She had been back several days when she met Corinna as she went off duty.

'You're back,' said that young lady unnecessarily. 'How are Marc and Emmie and the baby, and did you do anything exciting while you were there?'

'They're all very well. Marc is almost fit again— he has a governess, an awfully nice girl—Tine.'

Corinna, who knew all about Marc, and Tine for that matter, since she had a habit of ringing up her cousin whenever she felt like it, said chattily, 'You're off duty? Good. I'll meet you at the front entrance in twenty minutes and you can tell me all about it. We'll go to Chiswick and get Breeze to give us supper.'

She saw the look on Caroline's face and added kindly, 'It's all right, Marius lets me use his house when I'm off duty.' She patted Caroline's shoulder. 'Don't keep me waiting.'

She sailed away and Caroline, watching her go, reflected that it was easy to see that she was Mr van Houben's cousin; they both had the same air of expecting people to do what they wished and no questions asked. All the same, she went to her room and showered and changed into the navy and white dress and the little jacket, crammed her tired feet into the new sandals and went back to the front entrance. Corinna was already there, talking to one of the housemen, but she bade him a cursory goodbye when she saw Caroline.

'Are we going by bus or tube?' asked Caroline.

Corinna had lifted an imperative finger to a passing taxi. 'I never go on either. If there's no one with a car I have taxis.'

'How nice,' said Caroline rather feebly as they were whisked away from their dreary surroundings across the city to Chiswick, which seemed like another world.

Breeze opened the door to them and admitted them with unsurprised benevolence.

'We're dying from hunger,' declared Corinna the moment they were inside. 'Do you suppose that Mrs Breeze could find us a sandwich or something?'

Breeze allowed himself a small smile. 'Allow her half an hour, Miss Corinna; I'm sure she will find you something.'

He led them across the hall to the drawing-room and Caroline, gazing raptly at the charming surroundings, said in surprise, 'But Mr van Houben has a house in Amsterdam…'

'Well, of course he has—he has to live somewhere, doesn't he? Besides, that's his family home; this place suits him very well when he comes over here, and he comes very often. He has a nice little cottage in Friesland too.'

Corinna went over to the table by the window and examined the bottles and decanters on it. 'Pale sherry?' she enquired, and didn't wait for an answer. 'I dare say,' she went on carelessly, 'if Marius marries he'll get a small place in the country as well—it would be nice for the children.' She motioned Caroline to a small velvet armchair and gave her a glass. 'I wouldn't mind marrying an Englishman and living over here; on the other hand I know some very nice young men in Holland.'

Caroline sipped her sherry and murmured politely while she looked around her. It was a much smaller house than the one in Amsterdam but it was just as

charmingly furnished. She asked, 'Will you go back
to Holland as soon as you've finished?'

'I expect so—my family live in The Hague; I've
four brothers but they all live away from home,
they're older than I am. Have you brothers and sisters?'

'No, I live with an aunt.'

'I dare say you have a lot of friends.'

'Well,' said Caroline cautiously, 'I do know just
about everyone in the village. I've lived there since I
was twelve.'

'London must seem a bit grim…'

'Most of the time we're in the hospital, aren't we?'

Corinna, who spent most of her free time as far
away from the hospital as possible, agreed. She was
a good nurse, liked by everyone, and she never failed
to pass the various tests with the highest possible
marks, but once she was finished she had every intention of going back to The Hague and enjoying herself and then getting married. She was a pretty girl,
the somewhat spoilt daughter of wealthy parents, and
there were young suitable men enough for her to
choose from; her future was pleasant and secure. She
was a nice girl and warm-hearted too, and she said
now, 'I daresay Emmie will invite you back to see
Marc—they are undyingly grateful to you.' She added
carelessly, 'Did you see anything of Marius?'

'Your cousin? Yes, he came several times to see
Marc and he was at the hospital when he went in for

his tests.' Caroline had gone rather pink, although she spoke in her usual quiet way, and Corinna gave her a thoughtful look. A pity if this nice quiet little thing had lost her heart to him; Marius, as far as she knew, was immune from romantic encounters of a lasting nature. A pity; he would make a splendid husband...

Breeze appeared in the doorway to say that Mrs Breeze had prepared a supper for them and would they be good enough to go to the dining-room?

'Thank heaven, I'm famished,' declared Corinna, and urged Caroline across the hall and into the dining-room.

Breeze hadn't done things by halves; the table was laid with a crisp linen cloth, sparkling silver and glass, and there was a bowl of early roses at its centre, and Mrs Breeze had conjured up a splendid supper: chicken soup and cheese soufflé with a salad and ice cream to round their meal off.

'Won't Mr van Houben mind?' asked Caroline, drinking coffee in the drawing-room afterwards.

'Of course not—I'm his cousin, I can come and go as I please—I come here for my days off and when he comes over to England he takes me out.' She said suddenly, 'Do you like him, Caroline?'

A question that Caroline didn't want to answer. 'He's very clever, isn't he? I don't—I don't really know him; I mean, you know how it is at the hospital, the consultants and registrars and those sort of people don't have anything to do with the junior nurses.'

Corinna poured more coffee. 'Now tell me all about Marc when you got him home and don't miss a thing—he is such a darling, isn't he? So is the baby…'

Caroline answered as best she could, recounting in great detail the day to day activities at the van Houbens'. It was almost ten o'clock when Corinna said, 'Well, I suppose we must go back—I'll ask Breeze to get us a taxi.'

Parting company in the nurses' home, Caroline said, 'Thank you for asking me to supper, I enjoyed it very much.'

Corinna smiled. 'Good, so did I, and it was nice to catch up on the news. Goodnight, Caroline.'

Caroline had a bath and went to bed but Corinna went back to the hall of the nurses' home where there was a telephone. No one was supposed to use it after ten o'clock, but that had never bothered her. She made herself comfortable on a stool taken from Sister's office and dialled a number, and when she said who she was, 'You should be in bed,' replied her cousin Marius. 'I suppose you're short of money or worse—fallen in love again.'

'Don't be horrid.' They were speaking Dutch and she made no attempt to lower her voice for fear of waking anyone and them coming to see what she was doing. 'Guess who spent the evening in Chiswick with me…'

'My dear girl, I've had a hard day and I'm beyond guessing anything.'

'Caroline! Remember her—she looked after Marc.'

'Of course I remember her, she's only been gone a week.' He paused. 'She isn't ill?'

'Of course not—she was off duty at the same time as I was and it was an opportunity to hear about Marc. She's a dear creature, isn't she, Marius?'

'Marc was fond of her. It was largely due to her that he has made such a good recovery. Whether she is a dear creature or not I do not know.'

'Don't you like her?'

'My dear Corinna, I am quite indifferent to her, and now shall we say goodnight? I've a heavy day again tomorrow.'

'Poor Marius—so have I—up with the lark and run off my feet. *Wel te rusten.*'

She went back to her room, smiling angelically at one of the older sisters who had opened her door and was looking suspicious. 'Make a little less noise,' snapped that lady, and closed the door again.

Corinna took her time getting ready for bed while she went over the evening. Caroline had blushed when she had mentioned Marius and she hadn't said whether she liked him or not—and Marius had been equally evasive. She was fond of her cousin and had long ago decided that he should find himself a wife; she knew all about his earlier love-affair but that was years ago, and she had and so had his family, produced suitable young women from time to time in the hope that he would fall in love with one of them. He enjoyed their company, took them out—theatres and dinners and dancing—but he was still heart-whole. Could it possibly be, thought Corinna as she at last settled herself into bed, that they liked each other? A most unlikely pair, but Caroline was the kind of girl who would make a good wife, loving and serene and sensible and on occasion not afraid to speak her mind. Marius needed someone like that to go home to each evening. And soon, she thought sleepily, before he becomes a confirmed bachelor.

She and Caroline saw little of each other for almost a week; they were on different wards and Corinna was senior, with her own circle of friends and fully occupied leisure time. When Marius telephoned to say that he would be coming over to England in a couple of days, she had no chance to tell Caroline, and even if she had she wouldn't have said anything. If Marius wanted to see Caroline he could do so easily enough, but if he was as uninterested as he said he was then it would be kinder to Caroline if she knew nothing about his coming.

So when he walked on to the children's ward with Sister Crump two mornings later Caroline was taken by surprise. She had just come out of the sluice-room and turned round and went straight back in again, hoping that she hadn't been seen. She didn't think he would be in the ward long; it wasn't as though he did a round like Mr Spence. He had come to check on the small girl with the terrible cleft palate and double hare lip who would need careful anaesthetising; she should have thought of that.

She began to clean the already clean sink and a student nurse, only just on the ward put her head around the door.

'Sister Crump wants you,' she hissed. 'She's in the ward.'

With the greatest reluctance Caroline followed her, shut the sluice-room door carefully behind her and went to where Sister Crump and Mr van Houben were standing in the middle of the ward.

He looked her over carefully. 'Good morning, Nurse. You expressed the doubt that I would remember you. You see that I have. Sister Crump tells me that you have settled down again. I have just been telling her how very grateful my sister-in-law is for the care you gave little Marc.' He turned to Sister Crump. 'Perhaps we might have Nurse to special this little girl I've come to see—Shirley, isn't it? A difficult case which will need all our care and attention.'

'Mr Spence suggested that too; as far as I'm concerned, sir, it seems a good idea. Shirley will need all the patience there is for a week or so.'

Mr van Houben allowed his eyes to rest on Caroline, standing there outwardly meek and inwardly, he felt sure, boiling over because they were deciding everything without so much as a token request for her services.

'Good, good,' he said in an absent-minded manner. 'Then that's settled.' It had been settled between Mr Spence and himself previously—indeed it was he who had suggested it in the first place. Finally he added, 'We shall be obliged to Nurse—it may mean awkward duty hours and so on. You have a reliable night nurse, Sister?'

Sister Crump gave him a look implying that all her nurses were reliable.

'The child's going to Theatre at four o'clock. If you want Nurse Frisby to go with her, she had better go off duty…when are you off today, Nurse?'

'Five o'clock, Sister.' And she had planned a trip to a West End cinema with several of her friends.

'Change with Nurse Foster and go off duty at midday. We'll worry about tomorrow when we get to it.'

'Nothing planned for this evening?' asked Mr van Houben casually.

'Yes.' She was aware of Sister Crump's annoyance. 'Yes, sir, but it doesn't matter in the least.'

It didn't. They had met again—he was standing in front of her and he'd remembered her. The day was suddenly splendid; she would, if necessary, stay all night and all day with Shirley if he asked her to. Her grey eyes shone at the thought so that Mr van Houben, seeing their sparkle, decided that he had been mistaken in thinking of her as a plain girl.

'Shall we take a look at Shirley?' he asked, and
Sister Crump sent Caroline back to see to the ten
o'clock feeds. Which meant that she could think
about him while she bottle-fed the three babies one
after the other.

She went off duty punctually, leaving a cross
Madge Foster to do her work, and during the somewhat lengthy walk through the hospital to the nurses'
home had time to lose some of her euphoria. Just
because Mr van Houben had turned up, she had no
reason to get excited. He hadn't come to see her, and
in a way it was a pity that they had met again, for
she had been doing her best for ages to forget him.
Not very successfully, but with practice it would
probably be easier. She suited the action to the
thought and started to plan her few hours of freedom.
Never mind her dinner, she would get a sandwich and
a cup of coffee somewhere, but first she would take
a bus away from the hospital. Victoria Park was the
nearest green space she could think of. She ran down
the last of the stairs and almost overbalanced against
Mr van Houben's waistcoat.

He set her back on her feet. 'Ten minutes,' he told
her. 'I'll be outside with the car, don't keep me waiting.'

She gaped at him, her gentle mouth open. 'Ten
minutes—what do you mean? Outside—why?'

'Don't argue, there's a good girl. Just do as I say.

I have so many messages for you from Emmie and Marc and Tine, and neither of us has much time.'

Rather to her own surprise she heard herself say, 'Very well, I'll be as quick as I can,' and she sped away, racing through the nurses' home to her room and almost upsetting Sister on the way.

'Late for a date?' asked that kindly lady, dusting herself down while Caroline apologised.

'Yes—no, not yet, but I shall be. So sorry, Sister.'

It would have to be the navy and white dress and the little jacket, she decided as she tore out of her uniform, found stockings and sandals, made up her face in a sketchy fashion and pinned her hair into the french pleat. Nothing startling, she decided, peering into the small looking-glass, but it would have to do. Only a man would expect a girl to get ready to go out in ten minutes.

It had taken her a little longer than that but when she went outside into the forecourt he opened the car door and stuffed her in without a word. 'We can talk over lunch,' he told her, getting in beside her and driving away without fuss, into the stream of midday traffic, leaving the small houses standing in red-brick rows and the rather shabby little shops, crossing the city until they reached Chiswick.

As he stopped Caroline said, 'Oh—I came here with your cousin Corinna the other evening—she wanted to know about Marc and we happened to meet as we were going off duty.'

'It's her second home while she's over here.' He had got out and paused to open her door and Breeze was standing by the open front door ready to admit them.

'We're both hungry, Breeze,' said Mr van Houben, 'but give us ten minutes for a drink, will you?'

He sat her down in the drawing-room by the open window. The garden behind the house was small but full of colour and there were birds singing in the birch trees at its end. It seemed a thousand miles away from the hospital.

'Sherry?' he asked. 'Or white wine?'

She chose the sherry, and when he sat down in a large wing chair near her a ginger cat came in from the garden and sat down between them, washing himself.

'Blossom,' said Mr van Houben. 'Mrs Breeze's devoted companion, but he prefers the drawing-room if he can get in there.' He glanced at her with a smile. 'Your aunt has a cat—Theobald? A handsome beast.'

Blossom got up and jumped on to Caroline's lap and she said, 'Blossom is handsome too,' and was racking her brains as to what to say next when Breeze came to tell them that lunch was served.

Mr van Houben so far hadn't mentioned Marc or anyone else she had met in Holland, and it seemed that he didn't intend to for the moment, for he kept up a flow of small talk while they ate potted shrimps, lamb cutlets with creamed potatoes and tiny peas and carrots and then a glazed apple tart with whipped cream. Caroline, who had been very hungry, enjoyed every morsel.

'I think your Mrs Breeze must be a marvellous cook.'

'Oh, indeed she is.'

'Well, I do hope you tell her so from time to time, though I expect you do. It's nice to be appreciated.' She blushed then because it sounded as though she was asking to be appreciated too, for nursing Marc, and he watched the colour creep into her cheeks with amusement tinged with concern because she was upset.

'Don't we all?' he observed lightly. 'And you would be surprised at the number of patients I have had who take one's skills for granted and don't say thank you.'

'You find that?' She was astonished. 'I should have thought they would have been so thankful—I mean, quite a lot of them might have died because there was no one to give them a complicated anaesthetic.'

'I only hope that we can deal with little Shirley— has she good parents?'

'No. They left her with her granny—no one knows where they are now.'

'All the more reason to turn her into as pretty a girl as possible! Mr Spence is a wizard with a scalpel, you know.'

They were having their coffee in the drawing-room

before he told her about Marc. The little boy was doing well and Tine was a great success, although he still had brief bouts of childish rage. 'Emmie sends her love and hopes they will all see you again some time.'

'That would be nice.' Caroline wished she could think of something interesting to say. Actually it surprised her that she could talk at all, for just being with him was enough to render her speechless, which wouldn't do at all. She must at all costs preserve a placid front, just as though she hadn't the least interest in him. All the same, while they sat there and he kept a flow of undemanding talk going, she wondered about him. She knew all about his love-affair, but that had been years ago, Corinna had told her that, and from remarks Mevrouw van Houben had passed she rather gathered that he knew a great many people and any one of them must be the kind of woman he would marry—tall and graceful and always suitably dressed. She hadn't a chance, even if she were silly enough to try and interest him… She was sure he hadn't noticed her new clothes or the way she had done her hair.

Mr van Houben, rambling on about the pleasures of gardening, watched her from under his lids and felt a faint stirring of interest. She was quite different from any other girl he knew, and she was making no effort to engage his attention; indeed she was only half listening to what he was saying. He wondered what was going on inside that mousy head—there was more to the girl than one would suppose. He found himself thinking that it might be very interesting to find out.

He finally drove her back to the hospital and went in with her.

She stopped just outside the entrance to thank him. 'It was a lovely lunch,' she told him, 'and I did enjoy the afternoon. Thank you very much, Mr van Houben.'

He smiled down at her earnest face. 'The pleasure was mine, Caroline,' he told her, and he meant it.

CHAPTER SEVEN

CAROLINE saw Mr van Houben an hour later, only this time he took no notice of her except to request this or that as he began the delicate job of anaesthetising Shirley, a procedure which took all his attention, and when presently a theatre nurse came to relieve Caroline he dismissed her with a nod and a, 'Thank you, Nurse,' uttered in a cool, detached voice.

It would be late in the evening before Shirley would be back on the ward; Caroline made up the bed in one of the side-rooms, made sure that the equipment was in order and went to have her tea. The night nurse was to come on duty at ten o'clock that evening, and since Shirley would spend the first hour or so in the recovery-room Caroline helped around the ward and went to her supper at seven o'clock. The day staff had gone off duty and the two nurses who would look after the ward during the night were already busy tucking the children up for the night. Sister Crump was in her office, where Caroline knew she would stay until Shirley was safely back in her bed.

The child was brought back just after nine o'clock and by the time Sister Crump and Caroline had settled the unconscious little form and connected up the drip, attached her to the monitoring system and seen that all was as it should be, the night nurse had come on duty. Shirley wouldn't wake for some time, but when she did, Mr Spence warned, she would need very careful nursing. The nasal feeding tube was already in position and great care must be taken to see that it didn't become dislodged. The operation had been a success and later he would need to do some plastic surgery on the lip. He added irritably, 'A pity she wasn't referred to me sooner.'

Mr van Houben came next, pronounced himself satisfied with Shirley's condition, gave Sister Crump a telephone number where he might be reached should he be needed, and with a quite goodnight went away again, leaving Caroline to hand over to the night nurse and take herself off to bed.

She was tired, but not too tired to think about Mr van Houben before she slept.

She had little time to think about him during the next few days. Shirley was a difficult patient and, unlike a very small baby, aware that there was something wrong, yet not old enough to have things explained to her.

She was small and undernourished and looked far younger than her eighteen months. Caroline found it sad that the small creature had had very little love in her short life and easily forgave her for her tantrums and grizzling, but she made tiring work all the same.

Mr Spence came each day, but of Mr van Houben there was no sign. She thought that he might have gone back to Holland but there was no one she could ask; Sister Crump would tell her it was none of her business in her gruff way and the night nurse was a girl senior to her whom she didn't know well. It was a week before she met Corinna going on duty one morning.

'No time to talk,' said that young lady. 'I'm late again. Did you see Marius?'

'Yes—yes, I did, when he was here for Shirley's operation.'

'Pity he didn't stay longer; he had to get back for some meeting or other then he was off to the States… must fly.'

She sped away, and Caroline, her head full of what little news Corinna had given her, went on duty too.

She went to Basing for her days off and found Aunt Meg and Theobald very soothing to her troubled thoughts; it was easier to forget about Mr van Houben now that she was away from the hospital and the chance of seeing him again, and Aunt Meg's sensible observation that it was a good thing that she hadn't stayed in Holland too long, for it might have unsettled her, warned her that she was unsettled already and likely to stay that way unless she became her sensible self once more. She went back to the hospital full of good intentions, but since there was no sign of Mr van Houben she was unable to try them out, though she did fill her off-duty hours with activity: playing tennis on the hard court at the back of the nurses' home, going window-shopping with whoever of her friends were off duty, studying hard instead of dreaming; but even with all this she still thought of him before she slept at night, wondering what he was doing.

It was several days later that Mr Spence brought a new houseman on his round. A thin, tall young man who looked vaguely unhappy. He had nice eyes behind spectacles but his ears stuck out and his hair was unruly above a face which held no good looks at all, except that when he caught Caroline's eye and smiled tentatively she saw that he was really quite nice.

He came along the next morning, to take a sample of blood from one of the children, and she was sent to hold the child while he did it.

'You've just come?' said Caroline, stating the obvious for lack of anything interesting to say and wanting to put him at his ease.

'Two days ago. It's all a bit strange. I don't know London at all—I'm from Birmingham, doing a six-month course in paediatrics. Do you live here?'

'No, in a village in the country—not far away, though.' She had the small boy on her lap, his head tucked into her shoulder, his small hands firmly held, his jacket already rolled up. 'He'll scream,' she warned, 'but don't let it worry you, he'll be all right. I've a sweetie in my pocket for him.'

He looked as though he would be nervous and clumsy but he wasn't; true, the child screamed, but Caroline was quick with the sweetie and a cuddle and the screams dwindled into gulping breaths and then, when she blew into his small neck, chuckles.

'What's your name?' He was tidying up after himself very neatly.

'Caroline Frisby.'

'Robert Brewster.' He smiled; he had a very nice smile. 'I say, would you come out with me one evening? Just for a sandwich or something…' His eyes behind the glasses looked anxious. 'I don't know anyone…'

She wasn't sure if that was a compliment. 'Yes, I'd like that. I'm off duty on Friday evening and on Sunday, I'll call at the lodge on my way off duty—you can leave a message there.'

'I say, will you really—you won't forget?'

'No.'

There was a note for her on Sunday evening—would she be at the entrance at half-past six? There were no details; she got into the green-patterned two-piece, caught up a cardigan and went punctually to the entrance.

He was waiting for her and met her with a broad smile. 'I've an old car—I thought we might go to Regent's Park. Do you know the way?'

She said that she did as she got into the battered

Mini. 'There won't be much traffic,' she told him. 'Sunday is a good time to see London.'

He drove well, parked the car at a meter and suggested that they might have something to eat.

'That would be nice—I'm not very hungry,' said Caroline, thinking of his pocket. 'There's a café on the next corner outside the Park; I dare say it's open.'

It was. They ate beefburgers and drank several cups of coffee while Robert talked. He was lonely; he hadn't been in the hospital long enough to get to know any of the other housemen and he had no friends in London. 'The nurses are all so...' He paused and she wondered if he had been going to say pretty and decided not to, but he went on, 'I'm engaged to a girl in Birmingham.' He added ingenuously, 'She wouldn't mind me being friendly with *you*.'

She supposed that a left-handed compliment was as good as any. 'You must miss her very much. Once you're settled in and can arrange a free day you must go and see her, or perhaps she could come here?'

'Yes, I'll do that. You don't mind my telling you about her?'

'No. What is she like?' asked Caroline obligingly.

Robert had been waiting for that; he launched into a glowing account of his Miriam which lasted through coffee and Bath buns.

Back at the hospital he thanked her warmly for her

company. 'Could we do it again some time?' he asked.

'That would be nice. Do bring a photo of your Miriam.' She gave him a motherly smile—perhaps it was the unfortunate ears or the spectacles, but he looked as though he needed someone to look after him. 'Six months isn't long,' she added in a comforting voice. 'Do you plan to go on working in a hospital?'

'There's a first-class children's hospital in Birmingham, I shall try for a job there.' He beamed at the thought. 'We could get married...'

'A very sensible idea,' said Caroline, and wished him goodnight.

Over the next few weeks she went out with him several times; they had slipped into a kind of brother-sister relationship although the hospital grapevine would have it otherwise. She was on her way to the path lab with some specimens when she met Corinna who put out a hand and stopped her.

'I've been wanting to see you—messages from the family and news of Marc. What's all this romantic chat about you and our Dr Brewster? Out every night in that car of his—are we listening for wedding bells?'

Caroline laughed. 'What rubbish—of course not—he's engaged to a nice girl called Miriam—but he doesn't feel at home here so I go out with him and we talk—or rather he talks about her. That's all.'

'Out of sight, out of mind—you say that, don't you?'

'Yes, but he loves her. He's a friend—nothing more.'

'It's time you fell in love,' said Corinna, and blinked at the tide of warm colour which flooded Caroline's cheeks and added quickly, 'I fall in love every few weeks, you know; it's great fun.' She smiled widely. 'I'm late, as always, and so will you be. We must have another evening together soon.'

She was gone, running along the corridor, ignoring hospital rules.

Marius telephoned his cousin that evening to tell her that he would be coming over to London in two days' time. 'I'll take you out to dinner if you can bear with a middle-aged cousin,' he told her. 'It will be the last time, I dare say; you leave again soon now, don't you?'

'Yes, I'm so excited about it, I'm going to have a lovely holiday—out every night dancing...'

'You haven't done so badly in London,' said Marius drily. 'Is Caroline still on the children's ward? She wrote to Emmie but didn't say where she was working.'

'Oh, yes, she's still there,' said Corinna airily. 'She's due for a move soon, though.' She began to talk about something else; it had been on the tip of her tongue to tell him about Caroline and Robert Brewster but something had made her change her mind. Marius might have asked after her out of politeness; on the other hand, if he was interested, it might shake him up a bit to discover for himself that plain little Caroline was by no means on the shelf yet.

He arranged to call for her in two days' time, gave her the latest family news and then rang off. Presently he picked up the phone again. Emmie answered. They chatted for a while about Marc's progress. 'He's doing splendidly, but I was wondering if a visit from Caroline might be a good idea.'

'She writes almost every week and sends little drawings for him, and of course I tell her how he's getting on; so does Tine. We'd love to have her if she could get a holiday. Have you asked her?'

'No. It merely crossed my mind. I'm going over to England in a day or so; I'll see Corinna and probably I'll see Caroline too and see what she says.'

He put the phone down and applied himself to the notes on the desk before him but presently he pushed them away and Nep, watchful at his feet, wriggled nearer and uttered a hopeful bark.

Mr van Houben bent to scratch Nep's ear. 'Not just yet, old fellow. Do you suppose it would be a good idea to see Caroline again? It is a great pity that I am unable to forget her, for I have no reason to remember her except as a good nurse…'

Nep muttered gently and Mr van Houben went on thoughtfully, 'If I compare her with the other ladies of my acquaintance she is completely outshone; she is, after all, a student nurse, one of hundreds with whom I come in contact almost daily. Granted, she played a large part in getting Marc back on to his feet, but any good nurse could have done that.' He frowned. 'No, that is not true, she held on when others might have let him slip through their fingers. But I must not allow gratitude to colour my thoughts about her.'

Nep laid his chin on his master's shoe and muttered again and Mr van Houben said, 'I'm glad that you agree with me.'

He called for Corinna two evenings later and had just settled her in the Bentley and was preparing to drive away when Caroline and Robert came out of the hospital entrance. It was the tail-end of a lovely day and Caroline had put on her flowered skirt and the silk top and done her face and hair with extra care because she had been invited to have a meal with Robert and his Miriam, who had come to London on a short visit. She hadn't been too keen on going, remembering the old adage about three being a crowd and not fancying playing gooseberry, but Miriam had written her a letter saying how much she wanted to meet her, so Caroline had agreed reluctantly.

Mr van Houben took his hands off the wheel and sat back watching. He said casually, 'Caroline has a boyfriend?'

'Oh, Robert Brewster—he's doing a six-month paediatric course. From Birmingham. He's rather a dear.' Corinna took a quick glance at her companion; his face held no expression but she knew him well enough to know that that indicated that he was hiding strong feelings of some sort. She went on cheerfully, 'He's got a frightful old Mini. I hear he's pretty good at his job; even the great Mr Spence thinks well of him.'

They watched the Mini leave the forecourt before Marius drove away in his turn. He didn't mention Caroline again during the evening, and when they returned to the hospital the Mini was back, parked with the other staff cars.

'Shall I see you tomorrow?' said Corinna.

'I shall be here some time in the morning. There is that burns case they will need me to look at to see if it will be possible to give an anaesthetic.'

'She's in our ward—her mouth and throat are badly damaged but I expect that you know all about it.'

'Yes. I've talked with Mr Spence. We must see what can be done. Goodnight, my dear.'

He walked her to the entrance to the nurses' home and got back into his car and drove himself back to Chiswick. Breeze, silently seeing to the locking up and going to wish his master goodnight, observed to his wife later that Mr Marius seemed quite put out about something. 'Miss Corinna after him for some more spending money, I dare say,' he chuckled. 'We shall miss her when she leaves us.'

Caroline, happily unaware of Mr van Houben's arrival, got ready for bed, had tea with several of her friends and recounted the pleasures of her evening. 'A very nice girl,' she observed, 'just right for Robert. I like her. He's managed to get a week off at the end of the month so he can go to Birmingham and be with her. They're devoted.'

'What did you eat?'

'We went to a small restaurant behind Oxford Street. We had soup and steak and kidney pie and ices after—oh, and coffee, of course. I wasn't too keen to go but it was all right, they treated me like a sister, if you see what I mean.'

Her audience nodded, Caroline was a dear girl, they all liked her, but there was no denying the fact that her lot in life seemed to be that of faithful friend. They went off to bed presently and she put her head on the pillow and slept, first of all allowing herself a few loving thoughts about Mr van Houben.

He had spent a good deal of the morning with the burns case, conferred with the surgeon who wanted to operate and then made his way to the children's ward. Shirley, he had been told, was still there, ready to leave, but since her granny didn't feel she could cope with her efforts were being made to get her into a children's home.

Sister Crump was in her office, and so was Robert Brewster, writing up notes. He got up as Mr van Houben went in and Sister Crump said, 'Good morning, sir,—nice to see you—you'll be wanting to look at Shirley? This is Dr Brewster, he's on a six-month course…'

The two men shook hands and Mr van Houben leant his vast frame against a wall and observed in his calm unhurried way that yes, he would be glad to see the child, and he added, 'And don't disturb yourself Sister, I'm sure Dr Brewster will go with me.'

Shirley's cot was at the far end of the ward, and since she had just wet her bed Caroline was changing the sheets with one arm round the toddler propped against the cot sides. An awkward business, but the other nurse on duty was in the sluice-room and Shirley was grizzling.

She looked over her shoulder at the sound of feet and at the sight of Mr van Houben went first very red and then pale; he was a glorious surprise, but the unexpectedness of it had taken her breath away, so that for a moment she was perfectly still.

'Hello, Caroline,' said Mr van Houben at his blandest. 'I've come to take a look at Shirley.'

He leaned over and lifted the small creature out of her cot and Caroline said belatedly, 'Good morning, sir,' and finished off the cot, not looking at him or Robert.

Mr van Houben was very much at his ease; he went and sat on one of the low tables where the children played, and sat Shirley on his knee, and Robert went with him. Not a perceptive young man, he yet had the feeling that neither of the two persons with him was really aware of his presence, and Caroline was looking flustered. He coughed, and Mr van Houben turned his handsome head to speak to him.

'Mr Spence did a splendid job of work here,' he observed, 'and of course the nursing of such a case is all-important—no easy task as you can imagine, with the child's arms splinted to prevent interference with the wound and the great difficulty in feeding and preventing crying.' He had opened the small mouth with a gentle hand and was peering inside. 'Of course, Sister Crump is one of the finest ward sisters there is, and trains her nurses to her own high standard.'

Caroline had finished making up the cot and wished that she had something to occupy her. It wouldn't do to walk away and leave the men there; one didn't leave consultants on their own; on the other hand she felt a fool standing there doing nothing.

She looked at Robert but he was listening to Mr van Houben and presently invited to give his opinion as to the best method of feeding a child with a cleft palate; he ventured a few of his own ideas, during which Shirley was handed back to her with one of Mr van Houben's bland smiles.

She put the child back into her cot, arranged suitable toys and locked the cot sides, taking as long as possible until he said, 'Don't let us keep you, Nurse,' and dismissed her with a kindly smile.

It was fortunate that there was an outburst of tears from a small boy on the other side of the ward; it gave her something to do but unfortunately prevented her from hearing what the men were talking about. Presently they strolled away with a 'Thank you, Nurse,' uttered in her direction by Mr van Houben and a sidelong glance from Robert.

'What plans do you have for the future?' asked Mr van Houben pleasantly of Robert.

'I want to go back to Birmingham—to the children's hospital there, sir. They've more or less agreed to consider me and I could work my way up to registrar in time.'

'You wish to remain there?'

'Well, yes. We plan to marry as soon as I'm appointed.'

'Your wife will work too?' asked Mr van Houben smoothly.

Robert nodded. 'But only until I've got started; she's keen on paediatrics too.'

Mr van Houben's face was impassive. 'Then I must wish you every success—the work is very rewarding.'

They had reached Sister's office and Robert didn't go in. 'It's been a privilege meeting you, sir,' he declared. 'I hope we shall meet again at some time.'

'Bound to—I come here from time to time, although my main work is in Holland.' He nodded an amiable goodbye and opened the office door.

Inside he sat down on the edge of the desk. 'Shirley's doing well. How is Nurse Frisby placed as regards holidays? My sister-in-law wants her to go over and spend a couple of days with Marc.'

'Well, she is due for a move in a couple of weeks; she could have four days off at the beginning of next week and go straight to Casualty. I shall miss her; she's a good nurse. I retire in four years; she might very well get my job provided she stays on here. She might marry, of course.'

Mr van Houben withdrew his gaze from the view of the chimney pots and shabby roof-tops outside the window. 'It seems likely,' he observed. He got up. 'I'll get Emmie to phone Caroline. Does she know that she is to be transferred?'

'No—but I'll tell her.'

She watched him go. There was nothing in his manner to indicate it, but she had the feeling that he was in a towering rage.

Caroline, going off duty in the afternoon, looked to see if his car was in the forecourt. It had already gone; indeed, he was on his way back to the ferry and Holland.

Emmie van Houben phoned her that evening. 'Marc does want to see you again,' she begged. 'Could you come just for a day or two, so that he knows that you haven't forgotten him? Please, Caroline—we will send your ticket and meet you at Schiphol. Could you not explain to Sister Crump? She is so kind and understanding?'

'I saw Mr van Houben this morning…he didn't say anything about Marc.'

Emmie's surprise sounded very real. 'Did you? Well, I don't suppose he would—he's going to Brussels and then on to Rome.' Quite true, only he wouldn't be going for several weeks.

There would be no fear of meeting him, thought Caroline, something she longed to do but which common sense told her would be useless and upsetting. 'I'll ask Sister Crump in the morning,' she promised, and put the phone down. But Emmie didn't; she went back to the switchboard and asked to speak to Sister Crump.

Caroline was a little surprised at Sister Crump's willingness to let her have four days off at the weekend. 'You are going to Casualty next Wednesday,' she was told gruffly, 'so it will fit in very well.'

'Casualty? Must I? Couldn't I stay here for another few weeks, Sister Crump?'

'Good heavens, girl, you want to finish your training, don't you? You've done well here and we shall miss you, but you mustn't get in a rut.' She waved dismissal. 'Take Friday evening off—you'll need to pack and so on.'

Aunt Meg, when telephoned, thought it was a splendid idea. 'And take a pretty dress with you, love, I dare say they'll take you out.'

The weather was splendid, Caroline wore the navy and white and the little jacket and, mindful of Aunt

Meg's advice, packed the green voile two-piece and, after careful thought, the pink cotton and lace Laura Ashley dress she had bought in a fit of extravagance. Her ticket had arrived by special delivery and she left quite early in the morning for the eleven o'clock flight. Mevrouw van Houben had said that she would be met, and she had almost all her month's pay in her handbag; she had nothing to worry her. She had been sent a first-class ticket and had every intention of enjoying the flight. Which she would have done, if only she could have stopped herself thinking about Mr van Houben.

By the time she arrived at Schiphol she was wishing—contrary to all her good intentions—that he would be there waiting for her. Of course he wasn't. Bartus van Houben, beaming with pleasure, was there with the car, full of questions as to the comfort of her journey. 'We are all so pleased that you can come,' he assured her.

'I am delighted to see you all again—I only hope that Marc remembers me. He is well?'

It took almost the rest of the drive to Alpen-aan-de-Rijn for Marc's doting father to enlarge upon his progress, and when they arrived at the house she saw that he hadn't exaggerated. The little boy was walking steadily and he had gained weight; what was more, after the first few seconds he recognised her and rushed to be hugged and kissed and made much of.

'You see,' cried Mevrouw van Houben delightedly,

'he remembers you. Come in, Caroline, come in. You will wish to go to your room, but please come down soon and we will have a drink before lunch. Tine is even now there arranging the flowers.'

So Caroline followed Bep up the stairs and into the room she had had previously, and found Tine there, filling a bowl with roses.

'So nice to see you again,' said Tine, and flung her arms round her. 'I talk of you each day to Marc and he does not forget you, and we do not forget you either. He is now a well boy; Mr van Houben was here and he is most satisfied.' She had sat down on the bed while Caroline tidied herself and took off her jacket. 'Such a pity that he is not here to see you, but you meet in London?'

'Well, I see him on the ward…' Caroline poked at her hair in a dissatisfied fashion. 'I'm going to go to Casualty when I go back.'

'You will like that? And he goes there also?'

'Most unlikely,' said Caroline.

They went down to the drawing-room together and found everyone there—the baby and her nanny, Marc and his parents, and since it was an occasion to celebrate they drank champagne.

They sat down to lunch presently, with Marc between Caroline and Tine. He was excited but not boisterous, and he ate his lunch very nicely, chattering to Caroline as though she had never been away, and she answering him, as she always had done in her own language, neither quite understanding what the other one was talking about but perfectly happy to let matters rest as they were. He was taken away for his rest presently and Tine came back to join them in the drawing-room again. Mevrouw van Houben was full of questions. 'Corinna will be home very soon now; it is fortunate that she has not fallen in love seriously with any of the young men with whom she goes out. She will settle down perhaps and choose a good Dutchman. She is a dear girl but spoilt by her parents. And you, Caroline—do you have a serious young man? Corinna told me that you were friendly with a new doctor. Is he nice?'

Mevrouw van Houben had bent her head over her tapestry work and didn't see Caroline's face. 'He's just a friend…'

And Tine laughed and said, 'That is what everyone says when they are asked such a question. We have to wait and see, perhaps?'

'Perhaps,' said Caroline, unable to think of a better reply.

It was delightful to be back in the comfortable and pleasant life which the van Houbens led; Caroline went to bed that evening happily aware that they were really pleased to see her again and that they liked her. Marius van Houben had a nice family, she reflected sleepily; she supposed that he was in Brussels or even Rome by now, unaware that she was in Holland. Not that he would mind; he had treated her like a stranger—well, almost a stranger—on the ward, and he certainly wouldn't put himself out to see her while she was here. She tried to think indignant thoughts about him but it was too difficult, she loved him too much.

The van Houbens went to church in the morning, and since Caroline offered to look after the children Tine went with them. It was delightful in the garden; the baby slept and little Marc sat on a rug while she sprawled beside him, showing him his picture-book and struggling to read the simple sentences in it, and when everyone came back from church they sat around drinking coffee, carrying on a rambling conversation about nothing in particular. Caroline found it very restful; there was a lot to be said for the lack of Sunday papers in Holland; it made for idle hours spent in idle talk instead of silence and the rustle of the supplements.

Mr van Houben arrived silently, not coming out of the house through the french windows, but taking one of the narrow paths at one side. Caroline was kneeling on the grass, tossing a ball to Marc, her back to the house, so that his quiet, 'Hello, Caroline,' took her by surprise. She scrambled to her feet and lifted a pale face to his.

'Oh, I thought you were in Rome or Brussels.'

'Otherwise you wouldn't have come?' he said. His smile was gently mocking. 'We must contrive to be civil for an hour or so. I'm only here for lunch.' He picked up Marc and tossed him gently in the air. 'And how is the hospital? and your friend, young Brewster?'

'Busy, and Dr Brewster gets on very well with everyone.'

The blue eyes scanned her face. 'He should go far.' He turned away from her then to speak to his sister-in-law and presently sat down by his brother and became immersed in a discussion which kept them occupied until they went indoors for lunch. Over that meal, although the conversation was general, he barely spoke to Caroline.

It seemed that he was leaving for Brussels in the morning, staying there for several days before going on to Rome and not returning to Holland for the best part of two weeks, and Caroline, peeping at him discreetly whenever she had the chance, was suddenly filled with a recklessness quite alien to her calm nature. Before he went, she decided, she would ask him why he disliked her—no, that wouldn't do—'ignored' was a better way to describe his pleasantly casual manner towards her. They had known each other for several weeks now, never mind that she was a student nurse and he a well-known consultant. Never mind too, that she was head-over-heels in love with him; he would never fall in love with her, but at least they could clear the air and perhaps even be friends in a limited way.

They sat around talking after lunch and Mr van

Houben showed no signs of leaving, so that when Tine came down from the nursery to say that Marc was grizzling for a woolly toy he had left in the little summer-house Caroline offered at once to go and get it. She didn't hurry, for she was mulling over what she intended to say to him presently; there was bound to be a moment when she could speak to him. She found the toy and started back to the house. The drawing-room was empty and she hurried through to the hall, just in time to see the Bentley driving away from the open front door.

Mevrouw van Houben turned to smile at her. 'Marius had to get back—he leaves early in the morning. He asked me to say goodbye to you and also to wish you every happiness in the future.'

Caroline clutched the woolly toy to her as though it were a lifebelt and she were drowning. 'I hope he has a pleasant journey,' she said in a voice which didn't sound like hers at all. 'I'll take this up to Marc…'

Tine took one look at her face. 'You have had bad news?'

'No, no, I ate too much lunch…'

She gave Marc his woolly animal and stayed for a minute or two talking to them both, reflecting that perhaps it was best this way: no awkward goodbyes when her tongue might have run away with her and she might have said things that she would have regretted. He thought so little of her that he hadn't even wished to say goodbye or given her the chance to do the same.

She went back downstairs, and no one seeing her sitting there listening to the van Houbens' friendly talk would have known that her heart was breaking.

'So silly,' she muttered to herself, lying awake in her bed later, 'for he never gave me any reason to suppose he was even the slightest bit interested in me.' To prove it she got out of bed and turned on the light by the dressing-table and examined herself in its looking glass. 'You're a fool,' she told her reflection.

CHAPTER EIGHT

MR VAN HOUBEN drove himself back to Amsterdam with controlled ferocity and Fram, going to open the door as the car drew up, sighed at the sight of his inscrutable face. The master was in a nasty temper, no less nasty for being under control; he wasn't going to be best pleased to hear that Mevrouw van der Holle, recently widowed, attractive and making the most of the brief meetings she had had with him at other people's houses, was sitting in the drawing-room, intent on inviting herself out for the evening. She would be out of luck, thought Fram, closing the door soundlessly and informing Mr van Houben in a toneless voice that he had a visitor.

Mr van Houben bent to scratch Nep behind the ear and didn't say a word beyond a brief, 'Thank you, Fram. I'll ring when I want you,' before opening his drawing-room door.

Mevrouw van der Holle was a handsome woman in her late thirties; she had no children and spent a good part of each day keeping middle age at bay. She was skilfully made up and slim to the point of thinness; she dressed very well, too. She came to meet him as he opened the door, smiling charmingly as she offered a hand. 'Dear Marius—I have taken you quite by surprise? I was driving past and I thought how pleasant it would be if we were to have a drink together and perhaps spend the evening. You were always so good to Jan when he was alive—' she looked suitably sorrowful '—and you are a person to whom I can talk seriously.'

'How kind of you to say so, Mevrouw van der Holle, and to suggest an evening together. It is my misfortune that I am on my way to the hospital and shall be there for the rest of the evening and probably half the night. I just called in to let Fram know. I do hope he has taken good care of you.'

She pouted very prettily. 'Oh, yes, but is there no one else who can take over from you? On a Sunday evening, too; it is too bad that an important man like you has to work.'

'Unfortunately accidents and illness take no account of the time of day.'

He had remained standing and after a few minutes of general talk she had no choice but to leave as gracefully as possible, escorted to her car very civilly by Mr van Houben but without the hoped-for invitation to dinner.

He went back into his house deep in thought. He had, of course, no need to go to the hospital that evening; it had been an excuse made in order to refuse his visitor's invitation. There was no reason why he shouldn't have invited her to dinner, which was

plainly what she had expected; he knew her only
slightly, but she was an amusing companion and it
would have passed the evening. He sat down in his
chair and Nep, who had retired under a table and
growled softly at Mevrouw van der Holle, came and
sat beside him.

Mr van Houben bent to stroke him. 'It is a ridic-
ulous thing, but I find that I prefer to sit here with
you and think about Caroline. An absurd situation—
we hardly know each other and yet I feel I have
known her all my life, and what is unfortunate is the
fact that she appears to be perfectly happy with the
idea of a future with that young Brewster.' He sighed.
'Nevertheless, when I next go to England I shall see
her.' He glanced down at the little dog. 'Do you consider that I am too old for her, Nep?'

Nep's short brisk bark was reassuring.

The last two days of Caroline's visit passed pleasantly
enough; the van Houbens had many friends; there
were people to lunch, a picnic on the Monday and a
drive along the River Vecht so that she could view
its scenery and the old houses along its banks, and in
the evening more people came over for drinks, and
ample time to play with little Marc. She was glad that
she had seen him again, for he had made a splendid
recovery and he was happy with Tine. When it was
time to say goodbye she went with real regret; she
was unlikely to see the van Houbens again, and in-

deed it seemed to her that Marc should be allowed to forget her—she belonged to a period in his short life which he would remember only vaguely. She would write from time to time, she assured Mevrouw van Houben, and would never forget him or them. She went back to England laden with flowers and parting gifts without anyone once mentioning Marius van Houben, and she hadn't summoned up enough courage to ask. What would have been the point in doing so anyway? she asked herself.

Casualty was so different from the wards that it took her a few days to adjust to its ways. It was almost always full; old ladies who had tripped up and broken wrists or legs, babies who had been scalded by a carelessly placed teapot or kettle, toddlers who had poked beads up their small noses or into their ears, the victims of street fights when the pubs closed, neglected cuts, boils, poisoned fingers and drunks, and over and above these the street accidents. The nurses were frequently run off their feet, driven remorselessly by the senior sister, middle-aged, and domineering and never at a loss, however awkward the situation. There was a junior sister too, just as efficient but a good deal more pleasant to her staff. As for the nurses, there were several part-time staff nurses as well as two full-time ones and three student nurses, of whom Caroline was the most junior. She knew none of them well; seldom did Sister speak to her; she was sent hither and thither from one patient on to the next, for most of the time not sure what she was doing and, since the other three nurses weren't disposed to be helpful, muddling along as best she could and going off duty thankfully and wishing heartily that she didn't need to go back. Airing her grievances with her friends off duty, she was given a good deal of sympathy.

'We all know how beastly Old Moss can be.' Old Moss was the Senior Sister. 'She's been there for twenty years and can't imagine life outside Casualty—Sister Taylor's scared of her and anyway there's always a rush on down there—no time to be friendly.' Janey spoke cheerfully. 'Rush around with everyone else, love, and think about the good time you had in Holland.'

Caroline had been doing that already; not so much thinking about Holland as about Mr van Houben. He would be away from home and she wondered what he was doing. Working in a hospital? Being consulted? Giving lectures to eager students? What exactly would he be doing when he wasn't doing any of these things? The world, she reflected gloomily, was full of attractive young women, any one of whom would make a splendid wife for an eminent medical man.

'I wish I'd never met him,' she muttered as she cleared a dressing trolley, aware that she wished no such thing.

She had been back for a week when she had days off and went to Basing.

Aunt Meg's solid form looked safe and comforting as she got out of the train at Basingstoke and Caroline almost ran across the platform to hug her.

'Well, well,' said that lady bracingly, 'it's nice to see you again, love—it seems a long while since you were home, but that's because you've been in Holland.'

She led the way out of the station. 'There's a bus in ten minutes; we can just get it, I fancy. Only two days, I suppose? Well, that's better than nothing, and they say it will be fine and warm for the rest of the week.' She glanced at Caroline's rather pale face. 'You look as though you could do with some fresh air.'

The bus was half empty; the early evening bus had taken the workers home already and those who were staying in Basingstoke for a meal or a film would take the late evening one. Caroline and her aunt sat side by side, not saying much but pleased to be in each other's company. Something wasn't quite right, reflected Aunt Meg, and she hoped that Caroline would tell her what it was before she went back to the hospital. She was far too wise to ask.

It was the following evening before Caroline talked about her trip to Holland. It had been a lovely day and now, in the early evening, they were sitting in the garden at the back of the house with Theobald on Aunt Meg's lap.

'It was nice to see Marc so well,' observed Caroline, apropos of nothing much. 'He seems to have made a complete recovery, and Tine is just right for him.'

'He remembered you?'

'Yes—it was just as if I hadn't been away. I hope he'll forget me now, though—after all, he's still only a little boy; in a year or two he will have forgotten his illness, and that will be a good thing.'

'What about you? Will you forget him, love?'

'Oh, no. It was an experience, but it has nothing to do with my way of life although I enjoyed it.'

'The van Houbens will be eternally grateful to you,' said Aunt Meg in her sensible way. 'Besides, you will meet Mr van Houben at the hospital from time to time and get news from him, I dare say.'

Caroline said, too quickly, 'Oh, I am most unlikely to see him again; he wouldn't come to Casualty, and besides, we—that is…he…' she sighed '…I think he doesn't like me—he's always polite and kind but that's all.' She added rather wildly, 'We haven't anything in common.'

What has that to do with falling in love? reflected Aunt Meg, and made a soothing reply. For that was undoubtedly what was the matter with Caroline; she was of course unable to speak for Mr van Houben, but he had, as far as she knew, remained heart-whole until now and he must have had the opportunity to fall in love a dozen times with the kind of young woman Caroline was not, and apparently he hadn't. She was an optimistic soul; she gathered up her knitting, begged Theobald to get off her lap and suggested that they went indoors for their supper.

Two days' peace and quiet in Aunt Meg's company did a lot to restore Caroline's good sense; she didn't like Casualty but she wouldn't be there for ever, and once she had found her feet and didn't have to keep asking where things were kept she might even enjoy it, and indeed, after another week she was beginning to find that the work was to her liking. There was rarely a leisurely moment while she was on duty and there was no question of finding the work monotonous; she marvelled at the variety of people she encountered during the day's work and, since she was willing and good-tempered, even Sister Moss forbore from criticising her more than once or twice a day. And once the other nurses realised that she had no interest in the casualty officer they were disposed to be quite friendly.

It was a Sunday evening, half an hour short of going off duty, when a woman came in with three small children. Sister was in her office, Staff Nurse had the weekend off and the two nurses on duty with Caroline had gone to their suppers, for it had been an unusually quiet period and they could be brought back quickly enough in an emergency.

The woman came in slowly, youngish, dressed in bright cheap clothes, her hair badly in need of washing, and heavily made-up. The children were too thin, and ill dressed, and Caroline longed to pop them into a bath and then into bed with nice clean nighties.

She crossed to where the woman was standing. 'Can I help?'

The woman said belligerently, 'You're a nurse, aren't you? It's Tracey 'ere. 'Asn't been too well for a bit; now she's got a cough and don't eat—keeps me awake at night, she does—perfect little nuisance.'

None of the children looked particularly healthy but Tracey was easy to spot; she stood between the other two children, holding their hands, her pale face even paler by reason of her red-rimmed eyes, her small nose running.

'Come into this cubicle,' suggested Caroline, 'and I'll fetch Sister.' She put Tracey on the couch.

Sister Moss was writing the report and was annoyed at being disturbed, but she put her pen down and went to look at the child.

'Get her undressed and into a gown,' she told Caroline, 'I'll get the CO down to have a look at her.'

She went away and Caroline began peeling off the few clothes Tracey was wearing. They were very dirty, and she put them into a plastic bag and wrapped the skinny little body in a clean gown. The child would be admitted, she felt sure; her temperature was high and her breathing was far too rapid. Besides that, she had noticed faint brown marks on the child's body.

The CO, called from his supper, came within five minutes with Sister Moss. Caroline could see that he was tired and on the verge of ill temper and Sister Moss made things worse by stating firmly that Caroline would see to him as she had her report to finish.

The CO gave Caroline an impatient look, although he sounded civil enough. 'Well, what is it all about?'

Caroline didn't waste words: temperature, breathing, cough, brown marks and dirt were described in less than a minute as he bent to look at Tracey.

He stood up presently. 'Broncho-pneumonia and from the look of that ear she's got a nasty infection there.' He gave Caroline a quite friendly look. 'Smart of you to spot the brown marks—we'll have to admit her. Neglected measles with its complications.' He turned to the woman, 'Now, Mrs White—I want to know when Tracey was first ill. Did you call a doctor? And the other children…?' He glanced at Caroline. 'Get Sister to admit the child, Nurse. I'd better take a look at these two while they are here. Now, Mrs White…'

Sister Moss was snappy after a long day. She was crosser still when Sister Crump said they couldn't have the child until they had a side-ward emptied. 'You'd better clean the child up,' she told Caroline, 'and then wait with her until they are ready for her. The night staff nurse will be on duty shortly. Her junior can take over from you.'

So Caroline went back and started to clean up Tracey; it would take several good warm baths to get the child clean but at least she removed the grime from the small face and gently washed as much of her as possible. The child was too ill to cry and Caroline was relieved when the porters came for her. Her mother didn't go with her; the CO had persuaded her to wait with the other two children until the social worker could come and take them to a hostel. From all accounts the woman was incapable of looking after the children, both of whom were probably harbouring measles too; to let them return to what was almost certainly an unsuitable home was quite out of the question. Caroline thankfully left the social worker dealing with the problem and went off duty at last. She hadn't been relieved; there had been a road accident in and both nurses were fully occupied.

She had her days off the next weekend and went home thankfully. It had turned warm and Casualty had been busier than ever, so that most of her off duty had been after a day's work, too late to go to Victoria Park and get a breath of air. She told herself that she would make up for that over the weekend.

Aunt Meg gave her a critical look. 'You look washed out, love. I don't think that Casualty does you any good. Can't you get moved?'

'Only when they say so. It's been a bit hot indoors all day; I'll be fine after a couple of days here.'

However, by Sunday evening she didn't feel fine despite the hours spent out of doors. All the same, she declared that she felt much better and went back to the hospital, lay wide awake for most of the night with a headache and in the middle of an exceptionally busy morning fell down in an untidy heap, fainting for the first time in her life.

Several of the patients waiting to be seen screamed, Staff Nurse came running and the CO, emerging from one of the cubicles, scooped her up and put her on one of the couches.

She didn't say, Where am I? when she opened her eyes. 'So sorry,' sighed Caroline. 'So silly. I'm quite all right now.'

She was prevented from saying anything else because Staff Nurse had thrust a thermometer under her tongue. The CO read it. 'Any headache?'

'Well, yes.'

'Sore throat?'

'Yes.' She nodded, and, being told to do so, opened her mouth for him to peer inside.

'Koplik's spots—you've got measles. That child just over a week ago.' He turned to Staff Nurse. 'Nurse will have to be warded.' He looked down at Caroline. 'Had them as a child?'

'Yes. But not badly—I was about six years old, I think.'

'Well, Dr Wright will look after you.' Dr Wright was the senior medical consultant. 'I'll see Sister. You'll be as right as rain in a couple of days.'

She didn't feel well; she was taken to a side-ward on Women's Medical, helped to undress, and slid thankfully between the sheets to fall into an uneasy sleep at once, only to be roused to take antibiotic pills and be examined by Dr Wright, who was a nice old thing and called her 'little lady' despite the fact that she looked like a hag. She went to sleep again and didn't wake when the SNO came to look at her and, after her, at intervals and without permission, such of her friends as were able to gain access to the ward on some excuse or other.

Corinna heard of it during dinner and, being Corinna went to Women's Medical, walked boldly into the ward while Sister was in her office and went to look at Caroline. She was asleep still, her long hair loose from its plait, her face shiny with sweat, a blotchy red rash making her pale face seem even paler. Corinna stood looking at her for a minute or so and then, since Sister had just come on to the ward at the far end, went down the fire escape to the ward below where she was working, went to Sister's office and asked if she might go to her room and change her apron, as a patient had been sick all over it: Sister viewing her apronless person, agreed absent-mindedly, busy writing up patients' notes.

The nearest phone was in the porter's lodge and

she had always been on good terms with the head
porter. Besides, he knew that Mr van Houben was her
cousin and was an important man, even if he wasn't
a regular consultant on the hospital staff. Corinna dialed a number and waited until she heard Fram's
voice, when she asked him to fetch Marius.

'He's having his lunch,' objected Fram.

'It's urgent, Fram…'

'Now what?' asked Marius a moment later. 'It must
be something very urgent to phone me at this time of
day.' He sounded amused. 'What have you done,
Corinna?'

'It's not me—it's Caroline. She's ill. I've just been
to see her—she caught measles from some child in
Casualty—she looks awful. I thought you would want
to know.'

Mr van Houben was no longer amused. 'Very perceptive of you, my dear. How long has she been ill?'

'She fainted on duty this morning; she's warded.
Dr Wright's seen her.'

Marius sounded very calm. 'Good. Now let me see,
there's a theatre case this afternoon and an appointment in Rotterdam tomorrow at three o'clock. I'll be
over sometime tomorrow morning, probably early.'

'You'll never get there and back…'

'Easily—I'll charter a plane.'

Corinna was serious for once. 'You didn't mind me
phoning you? I thought, well, you have seen quite a
lot of each other while she looked after Marc.' She

tried again, 'What I mean is, if it were Fram or Breeze you'd want to know about them, wouldn't you?'

'You did quite right, Corinna, one should look after one's own.' He added in a kind voice, 'Don't worry, dear, she's in the best possible hands.'

They said goodbye and he went back to his lunch but after a moment pushed back his chair and declared that he was no longer hungry. 'I'd like coffee in the study, Fram. Miss Frisby is ill and I must make arrangements to go to England and see her.'

Sitting at his desk with the faithful Nep's chin on his shoes, Mr van Houben suppressed a natural desire to leap on to the first fast-moving vehicle there was and get to Caroline without delay and studied his schedule. If he flew over in the early hours of the morning he could be back in good time to get to Rotterdam by three o'clock.

'You see, Nep,' he explained to the little dog, 'I must go to her. I know she will have young Brewster to hold her hand but I must be sure that she gets the very best treatment.' He sighed. 'Is it not unfortunate that I should find myself in love with a girl in a million who already has the admirable young Brewster waiting to scoop her up and rush her off to Birmingham?'

He picked up the phone and set in train everything necessary to get him to the hospital by the next morning.

Caroline felt very ill and she really didn't care if

she lived or died, slipping in and out of fitful sleep, aware of being made to drink and swallow pills and of feeling far too hot. Her throat was filled with barbed wire too, and the various voices telling her that she should feel better soon did nothing to convince her that would be the case. She was aware of Dr Wright standing by the bed but she couldn't be bothered to speak to him, only dozed off again.

It was barely seven o'clock in the morning after an endless night that she opened her swollen eyelids and saw Mr van Houben standing there looking down at her.

'So there you are—and about time too,' she said, and closed her eyes again and was instantly asleep, suddenly convinced in her feverish head that everything would be all right now.

He had gone, of course, when she woke up again, and since she was convinced that she had dreamt the whole thing she didn't ask if it had been a dream or not.

Aunt Meg, neat in beige and not a hair out of place, was no dream, however. Caroline saw her sitting there when she woke again and this time her throat was bearable and she felt quite clear in the head.

'I thought it was Mr van Houben,' she whispered.

'So it was, love. But that was this morning, very early; he's gone back to Holland.'

'Oh—why?'

Her aunt chose to misunderstand her. 'He has his work like everyone else.'

'I feel better,' said Caroline and went back to sleep again.

Mr van Houben, back at his home again after his appointments in Rotterdam, went to his study and shut the door. He had, with a terrific effort, erased Caroline from his mind while he dealt with a particularly difficult case to be anaesthetised, but now he allowed himself to reflect upon his visit. The sight of her pale face blotchy with the measles rash, eyes puffed up and hair tied back, lank and terribly lustreless, had wrung his heart. He had wanted to pick her up and carry her off to his home until she was better and then marry her out of hand. The strength of his feelings for her left him speechless, so that Sister, standing beside him, had begun a résumé of Caroline's treatment, under the impression that something had annoyed him.

He eased a foot carefully from under Nep's whiskery chin. 'How could I have been so blind?' he asked the little dog, 'and now she had the worthy Brewster to care for her. In due course he will carry her off to Birmingham and he will be a good husband and father to their children, and because I shall encounter him from time to time—for undoubtedly in the years to come he will make his mark—I shall be reminded of her, even meet her again. I have only myself to blame, have I not?' He gave Nep a pat at his answering bark.

Then he added, 'The least we can do is to send her some flowers.'

He picked up the phone and ordered roses, lilies, freesia and sweet-smelling carnations and then he dialed again this time to Dr Wright.

His flowers were the first thing she saw when she woke the next morning and the sight of them made her feel better at once. Then Corinna, coming to see her despite the strict rule that no one was to go near her for fear of infection, poked her head round the door, declaring that she looked better. 'Who are the lovely flowers from? Surely not Dr Brewster?'

'They were here when I woke up…'

Corinna nipped into the room and picked up the card by the bouquet.

'They're from Marius. ''Best wishes for a speedy recovery''.'

'How did he know that I had the measles?'

Corinna turned innocent blue eyes upon her. 'No idea— Oh, probably he and Dr Wright rang each other about something or other.'

'How kind of him.' Caroline closed her eyes and went to sleep again. She slept a great deal, waking only to drink what was offered to her and to try and eat the minced chicken and junket and yoghurt presented to her at intervals. She wasn't hungry and she wanted to be left alone, but pills and potions were proffered every few hours and Dr Wright came far too often, accompanied by the SNO, and once, after a day or so, by Mr van Houben.

Caroline was still feverish, but awake after a refreshing nap, stared up at him and said, 'I don't need an anaesthetic…'

He looked down at her, unsmiling, and it was Dr Wright who answered with a fatherly smile, 'Mr van Houben is over here to give a lecture; naturally he wished to see you so that he could reassure Marc's parents.'

Of course that was his only reason for coming to see her. She felt the tears pricking her eyes and swallowed them back so that she was able to say politely, 'It was very kind of you to send the flowers. I'm really very much better.'

Mr van Houben studied her thoughtfully. Perhaps she didn't look quite as wrung-out as previously, but she still looked what in hospital parlance was described as poorly. The rash was fading to an unattractive pale brown and a high temperature had caused her eyes to sink into their sockets. They were as beautiful as ever and nothing could destroy the beauty of the curling lashes or the gentle curves of her mouth. Her hair was deplorable, though, and the tip of her nose was pink. Nothing in his impassive face allowed her to see that he found her enchantingly beautiful and that he was head over heels in love with her.

He said in his calm way, 'I'm glad to hear that; Emmie will be delighted to know that too. They all sent their love.'

He smiled kindly and went away with Dr Wright, and presently Sister came to see how she was and found her in tears.

'Tired you out, did they?' she wanted to know. 'Nurse shall bring you a nice drink and you just have another nap.'

She didn't sleep but lay with her eyes shut, thinking about Mr van Houben, and when she opened them again there was another great bouquet of flowers. Its accompanying card was lying on the coverlet under her hand and she picked it up and read it. It was from Bartus and Emmie, and to her annoyance she felt the tears welling into her eyes again; she had hoped that the flowers were from Mr van Houben. 'So silly,' she muttered. 'He's already sent some.'

The staff nurse, finding her in tears, scolded her gently, changed her nightie and sat her up in bed. 'Not to worry, now, measles often leaves you weepy. Your aunt's coming this evening for half an hour. Even though you feel rotten, you're over the worst.'

Caroline agreed meekly; she was over the worst of the measles, she reflected tiredly, but how long would it take to get over Mr van Houben?

Aunt Meg, coming presently, brought a brisk com-

mon sense with her which made Caroline ashamed of
her self-pity. 'Another week,' declared that good lady,
'and you will be allowed home—a week of good
fresh air will put you back on your feet in no time.'

Caroline assured her aunt that she was very much
better. 'You're a dear to come all this way—you will
take a taxi to the station, won't you? It can be a bit
rough around here in the evenings…'

'No need. Marius came for me; he has to see someone or other here and he will drive me back presently.'

'Is he coming up here to fetch you?' Caroline tried
not to sound eager.

'He said he'd send a message when he was ready.'

'Oh, yes—of course. How is Theobald?'

He was discussed at length and then Caroline said,
'I'm to get out of bed for an hour tomorrow; I'm sure
I'll be able to come home in about a week's time. I'll
get Robert to drive me down.'

Aunt Meg let this pass; she had listened to Marius
van Houben while they had driven up to the hospital
and had drawn her own conclusions. She began a
soothing chat about the garden.

Mr van Houben hadn't purposely avoided young
Brewster, although he had no wish to meet him, but
coming from the consultant's room he came face to
face with him.

The young man wished him a polite good evening

and Mr van Houben, well mannered even when not feeling like it, agreed and paused to ask how he was settling in.

'Oh, getting the hang of things, sir, in fact I'm liking it very much.'

'Good. You will return to Birmingham when you have finished here?'

'Yes—I hope to apply for a post there—a flat goes with it, which means that we can marry—we've waited almost two years...'

Mr van Houben, on the point of bidding him goodbye, paused. 'Two years?'

Robert Brewster looked sheepish. 'Well, we got engaged although I'd only just qualified—Miriam said that being engaged would give us a good solid reason for planning for the future. I must say that I miss her very much; in fact I wanted to give the whole thing up and go back to her when I first came here, but Caroline—Nurse Frisby, sir—made me stick to it. Miriam and I are everlastingly grateful to her for her friendship—the two of them get on like a house on fire—she's to be a bridesmaid...'

Mr van Houben registered a strong resolve to make Caroline a bride before that could happen, but beyond lending a sympathetic ear to his youthful companion's enthusiastic talk he said nothing, but presently parted with young Brewster, who went on his way reflecting that old van Houben wasn't such a bad stick, even if he hadn't much to say for himself.

As for Mr van Houben, he took himself off to Women's Medical where he spent five minutes charming Sister before going to the side-ward where Caroline lay, listening dreamily to Aunt Meg's soothing account of the garden's prolific crop of salad vegetables.

His, 'Hello, Caroline,' was uttered in a casual manner, but the sight of him sent the colour into her white face and he was pleased to see that. 'On the mend?' he asked cheerfully, and eyed her deliberately. 'I must say you do look more yourself.'

'I look a fright, so you need not pretend,' said Caroline peevishly. 'Aunt Meg said you weren't coming...'

'Otherwise you would have combed your hair and powdered your nose. Never mind.' He smiled at her in a kindly fashion and noted with hidden delight that her spirit was returning. 'Has the rash all gone?'

'Yes, and my temperature is down and I'm going home very soon.' She spoke snappily; he could at least appear sympathetic instead of being horrid. She wasn't sure that he wasn't secretly laughing about something too. What had possessed her to fall in love with such a tiresome man?

She wouldn't look at him, so she didn't see his slow smile, but Aunt Meg, an interested spectator, did.

'You'll be wanting to go home,' she said, and got to her feet. 'I'm so glad you're better, love. I'll come again in two days; perhaps you'll know when you're coming home by then.' She bent and kissed her niece and Mr van Houben watched her, debating whether he might do the same, but, much though he wanted to, he resisted the temptation. It wouldn't be fair; Caroline wasn't well enough to know her own mind for the moment. He could wait.

CHAPTER NINE

CAROLINE continued to improve; despite her small size she was healthy and strong and once she was pronounced fit enough to get out of bed she quickly found her feet, ate everything offered to her and slept soundly at night. Indeed, her progress was so rapid that Dr Wright saw no reason why she shouldn't go home and complete the good work there.

'Two weeks,' Caroline told Aunt Meg when she came to see her during the week. 'Sick leave, not holidays. I can hardly wait.'

Which wasn't quite true; the sensible part of her couldn't wait to get away from the hospital, the quicker the better, and perhaps by the time she got back Mr van Houben would have gone to Holland, for he was still in London, her various friends had told her that, but he had made no effort to come and see her and why should he? she asked herself unhappily while at the same time wishing to remain as long as possible on the ward in case he might visit her. Of course, he didn't. Aunt Meg came for her quite early in the morning, helped her pack a case after suitably thanking Sister and the nurses and offering the usual box of chocolates, and followed the porter carrying her case to the entrance.

When Caroline had asked what time their train was her aunt had been evasive. 'Oh, plenty of time for that,' she had declared, and went on to the business of stating her opinions on the hospital's surroundings.

'Well, yes, I know,' said Caroline, 'but there are masses of buses all day and the Underground isn't far…'

'No need of that,' observed her aunt as they went through the doors. Breeze was there, standing by an immaculate Rover. He bade her good morning, expressed the hope that she was well again, smiled at Aunt Meg, took the case from the porter and held the door open for them to get in.

Caroline hesitated for so long that her aunt was constrained to give her a gentle shove from behind. 'So kind of Marius,' she observed comfortably, 'lending us Breeze and his car. He kindly fetched me this morning.'

'Is Mr van Houben in London?' asked Caroline.

'Oh, yes, dear. Several engagements, I believe. What a busy man he is. Did he come and see you?'

'No,' said Caroline. She would have liked to add something to that but she wasn't sure what to say, and anyway she was saved from doing so by Breeze getting into the driving seat and asking if they were quite comfortable, and, if she was rather silent as they drove to Basing, her aunt made no comment.

The village looked charming, and, after the drab streets around the hospital, doubly so. The cottage gardens were full of flowers and the trees were in full leaf. Breeze pulled up sedately in front of the garden gate and Theobald came to meet them. Caroline scooped him up and he sat purring against her shoulder as they all went into the cottage.

'You will have a cup of coffee?' asked Aunt Meg of Breeze. 'And I baked an apple cake... I'm sure I can't compete with Mrs Breeze's cooking; I hear from Mr van Houben that she is quite splendid.' She ushered Breeze into a chair. 'And you sit down too, love, you mustn't overdo things for a few days. You have had measles, no doubt?' she addressed Breeze.

'Indeed yes, Miss Frisby, when I was a nipper, as you might say. A very nasty thing it is too. It is a great relief to us all that Miss Caroline has made such a speedy recovery.'

He didn't stay long and he didn't mention Mr van Houben's name once.

She had been home for four days and was already looking more like herself, with colour in her cheeks, and her hair, shining from frequent washing and brushing, tied back in a long pony-tail, and since the weather was warm and sunny she had spent her days out of doors and acquired a faint tan. Aunt Meg cooked wholesome food and made sure that she ate it, so that her person, rendered skinny by high fever, began to fill out nicely in all the right places, and although when she thought no one was looking her face was sad, she was bright and cheerful enough in her aunt's company. Now that she felt almost well again she began pottering in the garden, going to the village to shop for her aunt and even riding around on her bike.

'I feel marvellous,' she assured Aunt Meg. 'I'm sure I could cope with anything.'

'Or anyone?' asked her aunt in an offhand way, making it sound like a joke.

'Or anyone,' said Caroline, full of good resolutions. Now that she was away from any chance of seeing Mr van Houben, she told herself that forgetting him would be much easier; she reminded herself of this each day in the vain hope that if she did so Mr van Houben would gradually fade away. Of course he didn't.

He came on a Saturday morning, quite early, bringing with him Robert Brewster. Caroline, picking strawberries in the back garden, looked round to see who it was coming round the side of the house and jumped to her feet, upsetting the bowl of fruit.

She said the wrong thing, witless with delight and desperate to hide it. 'Now look what you've made me do,' she snapped.

Mr van Houben ignored the berries but Robert got down on his knees and began to gather them up. 'A pleasant surprise, I hope,' he said blandly. 'Good morning, Caroline; I have brought young Brewster to see you—such a pleasant day. ' He was smiling a little with an air of reproof.

'Oh, yes, well…how nice. Hello, Robert.'

If Mr van Houben had any lingering doubts about Caroline's entertaining more than a liking for Robert, they were put at rest. Nothing could have been more sisterly than her manner towards the young man.

She took the bowl from Robert and said with belated hospitality, 'Do come in, I'm sure you would like a cup of coffee.'

She started across the small lawn between the two men and her aunt, looking out of a bedroom window smiled. If she had been a betting woman she would have risked her pension backing Mr van Houben. She withdrew from the window and went downstairs to greet her visitors.

'Well, this is a pleasant surprise,' she declared warmly, 'and just in time for coffee too. You don't have to rush back, I hope? There's a farm chicken roasting in the oven and strawberries and cream— you'll stay to lunch?'

Mr van Houben, watching his Caroline's face, replied for both of them. 'That would be delightful. We both happen to be free this morning and young Brewster looked in need of country air.'

'Now isn't that nice?' declared Aunt Meg to no one in particular. 'Marius, would you get the chairs out of the garden shed? And perhaps Mr Brewster—Robert, is it?—would put the table under the apple tree? Caroline, get the cake that you made yesterday, will you?'

Sitting under the apple tree presently with the coffee-pot on the table and the cake—pronounced delicious—nothing but crumbs on the plate, Mr van Houben took stock of Caroline. If he had found her beautiful when she lay on her bed hot and cross and covered in blotches, he found her quite bewitchingly beautiful now. Her hair was tied back, glossy and thick, she had no make-up on, but she really didn't need any; the faint tan and her pink cheeks—rather pinker than usual since he was there—had given her face just what was needed to turn its ordinariness into near prettiness; her eyes sparkled and her person was nicely rounded. She was wearing a cotton dress, a simple well-washed one suitable for pottering in the garden, and her bare feet were thrust into sandals. He wanted to whisk her away and tell her how much he loved her, but he could see that she was still cross; it wasn't the time or the place. Perhaps he shouldn't have taken her by surprise like that.

He was partly right—of course she was cross; if she had known that he was coming she would have pinned her hair into its tidy french pleat, done her face and put on one of her new summer dresses. As it was she looked a fright. She could have wept with rage and love and longing.

She went to replenish the coffee-pot presently and Mr van Houben continued to make easy conversation with his companions, his face pleasantly attentive to what was being said, looking as though he hadn't a care in the world, and when after a while Aunt Meg suggested that Caroline should stroll round the village with their visitors while she kept an eye on the chicken he voiced his willingness to do so in just the right casual voice. Robert echoed him, so there was nothing for it but to walk down to the church. 'Norman,' explained Caroline, 'and there's a sixteenth-century tithe barn a little further on.' When they had admired the barn, she said, 'There's a splendid ruin too, a Saxon castle—it's in the Domesday Book and then it was Norman and after that a Tudor mansion—Cromwell beseiged it for years.' She paused. 'It's a bit far, I think we'd better go back, it's almost lunch-time.'

She had avoided saying anything much to Mr van Houben; now she asked Robert about his Miriam and what his prospects were, and that took them back to the cottage just in time to sit under the apple tree again and drink the sherry Aunt Meg kept for visitors.

Young Brewster had forgotten to be shy; the talk was light-hearted and over their meal it continued, largely due to Aunt Meg's and Mr van Houben's efforts, for Caroline had very little to say for herself.

Aunt Meg, watching him looking at Caroline from under heavy lids, drew her own conclusions. It was quite obvious that young Brewster treated Caroline like a sister—they were good friends and nothing more—but she felt sure that her niece and this quiet, self-possessed Dutchman shared deeper feelings.

Caroline, for some reason known only to herself, was treating him with decided coolness, and he—he was secretly amused by it. Why? thought Aunt Meg, offering coffee. He looked almost smug…

It appeared that they had no need to return until the early evening, and since the pair of them offered to wash the dishes Aunt Meg was constrained to invite them to stay for an early tea.

Sitting comfortably in a basket chair under the apple tree, listening to the subdued sounds of washing-up, she remarked casually to Caroline, 'How pleasant to have such nice visitors—I was afraid you would find it dull here after hospital life. Robert is a pleasant lad—a slave to Marius, of course. Such a good man—Marius, I mean—not young any more…'

'He's nowhere near forty,' said Caroline quickly, not looking at her aunt.

'Good heavens, no—he's in his prime—it is a pity you don't like him, dear.' She sounded gently guileless.

'But I do, I do.' She gave her aunt a beseeching look. 'Please, Aunt Meg, don't let's talk about him.'

'Well, of course we won't if you don't want to, although personally I should like to get to know him better. Such a pity that he lives in Holland, and anyway, he told me that he has been asked to lecture in one of those South American countries—quite a long tour. Chile, was it? Or perhaps it was Colombia. Anyway it's a long way away. A good thing he isn't married.' She looked up to watch the two men coming to join them. 'How very nice to have the washing-up done for us—you didn't find it too tiresome?'

Mr van Houben, who had never washed up in his life before, assured her that it had been no trouble at all. 'Although I dare say we've put everything away in the wrong cupboards and drawers.'

'Never mind that, it will make laying the table all the more interesting. The grass is quite dry if you want to lie on it and take a nap.'

He took her at her word and stretched his vast person in the shade and closed his eyes, and presently Robert said quietly, 'He was up for most of the night; he was called in to anaesthetise a girl who had had her throat cut—very difficult.'

'So I should imagine. What time do you have to be back?'

'I'm on call from six o'clock. Mr van Houben is going out to dinner...' A remark which sent Caroline's imagination into overdrive. Naturally he would know any number of people in London—and by people she really meant women; she had him partnered with a glamorous blonde in no time at all, eating a delicious meal at a fashionable restaurant and going on elsewhere to dance and then driving the beauty back in his Bentley...

'Are you asleep, love?' asked Aunt Meg, 'If you're not, could you make some scones for tea? And there's that fruit loaf...'

Caroline was quite glad to go into the kitchen and gather together what she would need. The oven turned on to warm up, she made her dough and rolled it out before cutting it into neat rounds with the pastry cutter. While they were baking she could cut the loaf and butter it and lay a tray—it was too nice to come indoors, and as she worked she allowed her thoughts to wander, as usual, to Marius van Houben. Chile, or wherever it was, was a long way away and he would be gone for a long time, she supposed. At least while he was in Holland he could come over to England easily and there would always be the chance that she would see him now and then. Not that that was of much use, she reflected sadly, what with his indifference and glamorous blondes all over the place.

She arranged her scones in neat rows on the baking tray, put it in the oven, started to wash up—and became aware that he was standing in the doorway.

He didn't say anything, so she carried on, casting around in her head for a suitable remark to make.

'Why were you cross?' he asked mildly.

It didn't enter her head to pretend that she didn't know what he meant.

'I hadn't done my face or my hair and I'm wearing an old dress… I wasn't expecting you—anyone…'

'My dear girl, I hardly noticed.'

She was scrubbing the rolling-pin with enormous vigour. 'Oh, I know that.' She wrung out the dishcloth quite viciously and emptied the sink.

'So why should you be vexed?' he wanted to know.

She wasn't going to answer that, instead she said in a stony voice, 'Aunt Meg told me that you are going to Chile. How very interesting.'

'Colombia, actually.'

'I expect you will meet some interesting people.'

'We may not see each other for some time.'

He was leaning against the door, his eyes on her face, so that she turned away to busy herself with seeing if the scones were ready. He had put into words what she already knew; it made it very final.

'Well, yes, I suppose so.' She turned round to face him. 'But that's not important, is it? I mean...' She stopped. It was quite impossible to tell him what she meant.

'You mean?' he prompted.

'Oh, nothing.' She started to slice the fruit loaf. He took the knife from her. 'I'll do that. How delicious these scones smell. It really is most kind of your aunt to let us spend the day. Young Brewster is enjoying every minute.'

She buttered the slices as he cut them. 'Why did you bring Robert?'

'Oh, I wanted to be sure about something.'

She gave him a puzzled look. 'About his work? He's very keen. I do hope he gets that job in Birmingham so that he can get married to his Miriam.'

'I can't see why he shouldn't. He's proving very satisfactory, I hear. You'll miss him?'

'Me? Well, it was nice to have a friend.' She added awkwardly, 'I—I don't go out very much.'

He cut the last of the loaf, took the butter knife from her and took her hands in his, bent his head and kissed her on her astonished mouth.

'Oh,' said Caroline, 'why did you do that? Is it because you're going away—a kind of goodbye?' She was pleased to hear that her voice sounded normal, although she felt as if she had had an electric shock.

She would never know; Robert, anxious to give a helping hand had come into the kitchen intent on carrying trays. Mr van Houben handed him the bread and butter plate and then picked up the tea-tray. 'I'll be back to fetch the scones,' he said.

She had made the tea and taken the scones out of the oven, and was on her way to the apple tree with a dish of jam and a pot of cream for the scones before he returned, and during tea, although she joined in the talk with rather more liveliness than usual, she didn't actually speak to him.

They went directly they had had their tea, their offer to wash up again firmly refused by Aunt Meg. Robert had given Caroline a brotherly pat on her shoulder and reminded her that he would look out for her when she got back to the hospital, but Mr van Houben had bidden her goodbye in a vague and casual manner completely at variance with the kiss he had given her. Watching the car slide away from the gate, she reflected that he was probably an expert at kissing. She had from time to time been kissed, mostly medical students who had just passed their exams or had good news of some sort and were prepared to kiss anyone who happened to be there, but none of them had prepared her for Mr van Houben's expert performance. For that was what it had been, she was sure about that.

She filled the rest of the two weeks with hours of activity, gardening and biking, taking her aunt to Basingstoke to shop, walking old Mrs Tremble's pug dog while she spent a day or two in hospital, shopping and helping with the church jumble sale. Aunt Meg said nothing, only made cheerful conversation about the possibility of future holidays and enlarged upon the pleasures in store once Caroline had taken her final exams. Caroline went back to the hospital determined to let common sense take over from daydreams.

A good thing too, for she found herself back in Casualty once more, run off her feet, for the tourist season was in full swing and although the hospital wasn't in an area frequented by visitors to London there was a lot more traffic in the city and more careless driving, causing an unending stream of street accidents. There was a sprinkling of more adventurous tourists who wished to explore the East End and rather unwisely had chosen the evenings in which to do so, when they were a splendid target for muggers and youths out to make mischief.

After the peaceful orderliness of Basing, Caroline found it tiring and sometimes a little frightening. Casualty, thought of by a great many people as dramatic and exciting, was in reality gruelling hard work and sometimes sad. She did all her work as well as she was able and, with her being a kind girl, the patients liked her, and since she did her fair share the other nurses liked her too. Even Sister Moss, never known to praise, forbore from grumbling at her, although this didn't prevent her from telling Caroline that since she had returned to work on a Tuesday she need not expect her days off until the end of the following week. The off duty, she pointed out was already made out and there was no point in altering it. Caroline had just had two weeks' holiday anyway.

Caroline would have liked to remind Sister Moss that it hadn't been a holiday but sick leave, but she decided prudently to keep her tongue.

She had to admit after the first few days that there was something to be said for Casualty after all; it kept her mind off Mr van Houben, at least while she was at work. Off duty it was another matter; even at the cinema on an evening out with some of her friends his face loomed large before her eyes, so that the film became meaningless.

Two days after her return she met Corinna. 'Better?' enquired the Dutch girl. 'I must say you gave everyone a fright. Emmie phoned last night and she wanted to know if you were back at work. I must tell her that you are, although you still look a little off colour.'

'I'm fine.' Caroline cast discretion to the winds. 'Has Mr van Houben gone to Colombia yet?' She regretted the words the minute she uttered them. 'My aunt mentioned it.'

'Marius? He does get around, doesn't he? Time he settled down and took an interest in a wife and children—I'm always telling him that. He had better be around for the party I'm having when I get back home—only a few weeks now. I bought the most divine dress last week—there's a lovely boutique behind Harrods—I shall look quite beautiful in it.'

She beamed at Caroline, stating an established fact without a trace of conceit. Caroline said that she was sure she would look lovely and if she stayed talking any longer Sister Moss would kill her.

'You don't like it on Casualty?'

'It keeps me busy. Please thank Mevrouw van Houben for her good wishes when you hear from her again.'

'And love to Marc, of course.'

'Oh, of course. I'll never forget him.'

'I don't suppose you'll forget Marius either, will you?' asked Corinna, so unexpectedly that Caroline went red. 'He's not easily forgettable, is he?'

'I must go,' gasped Caroline. 'Sister Moss…'

She fled, ignoring the rule that no nurse ever ran except for fire and haemorrhage, and she found Sister Moss waiting for her.

'Why have you taken so long to fetch the films from X-Ray?' she demanded. 'Mr Stone is getting very impatient. Take them to him at once and then go along to the end cubicle—there's a carbuncle waiting to be dressed.'

Caroline, going in search of the owner of the carbuncle, reflected that life must be strange to Sister Moss if she saw everyone as an accident or a surgical condition. The carbuncle's unwilling owner was an elderly man with a patient face and a shocking smoker's cough.

'I dare say you smoke a great deal,' observed Caroline in her friendly way.

'Be the death of me, Nurse,' said the man cheerfully.

She changed his dressing, gave him some mild advice about his cough, aware that he would take no notice, and he went on his way.

'I 'opes I gets you next time,' he observed as he went. 'Yer don't nag.'

Caroline was to have the following Saturday and Sunday off and she began to think that they would never come; she was quite sure that once she was away from the hospital she would find it easier to forget Mr van Houben, something she was finding it extremely difficult to do. With all the goodwill in the world she was unable to stop herself from wondering what he was doing, and since this was before she slept, naturally enough she pictured him with a variety of young ladies, handsome creatures, splendidly dressed, with a witty flow of conversation to keep him amused.

'Oh, well, who cares?' said Caroline on Thursday evening, climbing into bed. 'Tomorrow evening I'll be going home.' She curled up in bed. 'I wonder what he's doing?'

Mr van Houben, a man who believed in getting things done once he had made up his mind to something, was giving his registrar lengthy instructions before booking himself and his car on to a midday hovercraft from Calais. He had discovered from Corinna that Caroline would be free at the weekend and would be going home on the Friday evening and he planned to get to the hospital during the late afternoon. That done to his satisfaction, he picked up the receiver and dialled the hospital, had a lengthy conversation with the SNO and then dialled in turn the various hospital governors. Finally he put the phone down and sat back in his chair.

'I hope and expect that the future, both yours and mine, Nep, will be an exceedingly happy one. I do not dare to contemplate otherwise.'

Nep gave a small, encouraging bark.

On Friday afternoon there was still an hour to go before Caroline could go off duty. Sister Moss was in her office and two nurses on duty with her were at the other end of Casualty strapping a sprained ankle. Caroline tidied the cubicles, collected the used linen and began to arrange the clean paper sheets on the couches. She was busy with the last one when she stopped to listen. Someone was coming through Casualty towards her, unhurriedly, and she knew who it was.

She turned round in time to see Mr van Houben draw aside the curtain and then lean negligently against a wall. His, 'Hello, Caroline,' was uttered with breezy friendliness.

'Hello,' said Caroline and, since she was finding it difficult to speak, she stood staring at him.

Mr van Houben rattled the loose change in his pocket. 'Ready to go off duty?' he enquired pleasantly.

She nodded again. Then, as the silence lengthened asked, 'Shall I fetch Sister?'

'No,' he smiled then, a smile of such gentleness and love that she actually took a step towards him and then paused to ask,

'What do you want?'

'You,' said Mr van Houben.

She went a little pale. 'Oh, no—I mean, I expect I'm just a passing fancy...'

'My dear, darling girl, most certainly I fancy you, I have indeed fancied you for some time and have no doubt of it, I shall continue to do so for the rest of my life. Moreover I'm in love with you, and life without you does not bear contemplation.'

For such a big man he moved very swiftly, and she found herself crushed against his waistcoat and told to look up.

She would have to anyway, for she could hardly breathe, her nose buried in clerical grey cloth. 'That's better,' observed Mr van Houben, and after a moment studying her face kissed her gentle mouth. He took his time, pausing just long enough to ask, 'Will you marry me, my little love?' before kissing her again.

Presently Caroline said, 'Yes, Marius, I will, for I love you too. Only I've thirteen months' training to finish.'

He took off her cap and kissed the top of her head. 'I've dealt with that,' he told her. 'You can leave as from now, with the blessing of the board of governors and the SNO. We must mention it to Sister Moss as we go.'

'She'll never allow me to leave,' began Caroline.

'Don't be a goose, my darling. Put on your cap for the last time and come with me.'

She did as she was told, for there seemed no point in not doing so. She gave a final pat to the paper sheet on the couch and went with him through Casualty to Sister's office.

Mr van Houben had her by the hand and he made

no effort to relinquish it. He met Sister Moss's astonished face with a bland smile.

'Nurse Frisby and I are to be married,' he observed
in a voice as bland as his smile. 'She is leaving as
from today, with the full permission of the board of
governors.'

Sister Moss rose from her chair, her complexion
dangerously puce.

'I never heard of such a thing…'

'Well, no, I grant you that it is rather unusual, but
the board of governors…'

'*You're* on the board, sir,' observed Sister Moss
awfully.

'Indeed yes, Sister. You will wish us happy?'

'I don't know what the world is coming to. In my
day…' She suddenly looked so forlorn that Caroline
leant forward and kissed her cheek. 'I hope you will
come to our wedding,' she said.

Walking along the gloomy passage which connected Casualty with the rest of the hospital, Caroline
said, 'I hope you don't mind—my asking Sister Moss
to our wedding, I mean.'

He stopped to take her in his arms again. 'Ask the
entire hospital staff if you wish, my love, only don't
waste too much time over it. A week or two…'

'I've nothing to wear—Aunt Meg—and where will
we live?'

He brushed away a few untidy wisps of hair and
tucked them under her cap. 'Why, in Amsterdam, of

course. I promised Nep I would bring you back as soon as possible. Shall we go and see Aunt Meg and then come back to Chiswick? I've an appointment with a rather worthy bishop in the morning—I thought a special licence?'

He smiled down at her. 'Think of poor Nep waiting so patiently.'

'You had it all arranged…?'

'Oh, yes.'

'Supposing I had said no?'

'I would have thought of something else.'

She reached up and kissed him. 'There's no need for that. I said yes.'

MILLS & BOON®

*M*akes
any time
special

Enjoy a romantic novel from
Mills & Boon®

Presents...™   *Enchanted™*   TEMPTATION®

Historical Romance™   ⊣ MEDICAL ROMANCE™

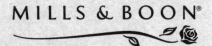

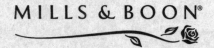